COME WALK WITH ME THRU THE NEEDLE'S EYE

A Biography of Irma Davis, Founder of the Needle's Eye

by

Irma Davis

with

Celia Lehman

Cover Design by Gloria Jean Robbins

ISBN; 0-936369-43-4
© 1991 Irma Davis
SonRise Publications and Distribution Company
Route 3 Box 202, New Wilmington, PA 16142
Printed in U.S.A.

Acknowledgements

When Irma asked me to help her write this story I was not willing to do it until I had clear directions from the Lord. The first test was to get a publisher before writing the script.
   The answer came while I attended the St. Davids Christian Writers' Conference near Philadelphia. Representatives from various publishing companies came to the week-long session to request types of books they wished to publish. I prayed each day for a lead to the Needle's Eye story. Sunday, Monday, Tuesday passed but there were none. When Wednesday came I was jolted from my chair when a representative asked for a book with a solution to one of America's problems (such as alcohol or drug abuse) in the form of a biography. That was Irma Davis' story!
   Irma and I worked together to compose the book but when we saw the immensity of the task, we were not sure we would continue. At that moment the unlit candle on the table where we were sitting, suddenly burst into two flames. We took it as an omen from the Lord that He wanted us to continue the project.
   Unforeseen difficulties loomed on the horizon. The publishing company who promised to publish our book suddenly had to forgo the contract due to financial difficulties. When we finally secured another company the type setter could not read the words because a misdirected computer had deleted one letter from each word in the manuscript.
   The first acknowledgement, therefore, goes to God who

gave us insight and persistence.

Both of us want to thank our families for putting up with time we put into our book instead of spending it with them. Irma would like to dedicate the book to her husband Bob who saw the dream with her and to her children Robert Jr., Ronald and Marilyn Lane along with their spouses and children, and to the staff at the Needle's Eye. They encouraged her to continue working when she was sick and drove her to where she needed to go.

Celia appreciated her husband Calvin's prayers for guidance and for putting up with the late pecking on the computer at night. She wishes to thank her sister Ruth Gerber who took over many duties to give Celia time to work on the book. Barbara Hodel gave many helpful suggestions as did Joanne Lehman and Frieda Amstutz when they proofread the manuscript; and a heartfelt thanks to Steve Dunham for editing the final draft.

Delores Smith furnished material for chapter three; Gary Hamm's information is found in the last chapter. Special thanks to Gloria Jean Robbins for designing the cover. For these we are grateful.

Pastor Bill Detweiler laid hands on the script and prayed for its success before it went to the publisher, and last but not least, Florence Biros, a sister-in-the-Lord took the initiative to get it into print.

Without these people we never would have made it.

>	Irma Davis,
>	Celia Lehman
>	September 7, 1991

Preface

Come with me. I'll take you to a place that unburdens people of their load of sin and despair and gives them life and hope through Jesus Christ.
If you are sensing a need for help or are overwhelmed by peoples' cries for answers to a problem whether it be sin, drugs or alcohol, this book is for you. It has practical, down-to-earth suggestions that, if followed, will bring about a change.
There are many kinds of burdens. Drug abuse is one. It has been named America's number-one problem. One out of four high school students has tried cocaine; frequent use has doubled. Congressmen are getting concerned enough to allocate eight billion dollars to fight a war against drugs. It is the first time in American history that a national drug strategy has been attempted in a comprehensive program to wipe out the problem.
It seems appropriate at such a time to focus on a program that has been highly successful both in its prevention of and holistic approach to chemical dependency. The Needle's Eye, a redemptive Christian counselling center located in the Southside of Youngstown, Ohio, was started by black leader Irma Davis. This modern Queen Esther is willing to give her life to save her people from the bondage of drugs and alcohol abuse. She introduces them to Jesus Christ, the true liberator; she counsels them and directs them to proper channels to get further help.
Her ratio of success in finding answers for treatment of addiction in a black community has gained national recognition.

In May of 1987, she responded to an invitation from First Lady Nancy Reagan, and attended the "Just Say No" program at the White House.

In 1986, when Governor Celeste set aside November as "Alcoholic Month," she was instrumental in starting a prevention program that included youth in a parade denouncing drugs in Youngstown.

At the time of this writing, two other models, one in Baltimore, Maryland, the other in Newport News, Virginia, have proven successful in patterning their program after the Needle's Eye in Youngstown, Ohio. Others are following suit.

All scenes in the book are authentic; however, the names of the people who are being helped have been changed to protect their identity.

Do you want to see how lives were changed? How your life can change? Come with us; Walk Thru the Needle's Eye!

Introduction

The lights went out.
Then a frightening siren, signaling an air raid, spread through the large ballroom of the Pittsburgh Hilton, where 1,500 college students had gathered for a conference entitled Jubilee 1988.
As the piercing vibrations echoed through the hallway, students cast uneasy glances, their spines straightening for an announcement. They waited; then a voice broke through.
"You are about to be thrust into an encounter you will not soon forget. Today you will be given an opportunity to examine the Lordship of Christ in your life. It will be your responsibility to learn how to step out in the power of the Holy Spirit to work for the redemption of every person on earth, not excluding the black people of the ghettos."
The students breathed more easily as the announcements explained the choices of seminars being offered.
The crowd dispersed to assemble at various locations. Thirty students chose to hear Irma Davis on the topic "The Black Family; Confronting the Issue." Little did they realize they were about to meet a modern Harriet Tubman! But instead of freeing people from slavery through the Underground Railroad, Irma Davis had worked actively the past twenty years to free people bound to drugs and alcohol.
As the students poured into her room, the tall, forceful

black woman flashed a big smile. An aura of light seemed to encircle her face, lighting up one tough woman. She's had to be tough to be the founder and director of the Needle's Eye, a Christian counselling center in the south side black community in Youngstown, Ohio--a city with the reputation of having a higher percentage of cocaine users than any other small city in the United States.

Even before the last students entered she was addressing the group. "I see blacks in this audience. Good to see you. Blacks add color to a crowd!

"Move in, move in. We have room for all of you," she urged as more students arrived.

A college professor gave the formal introduction."Irma Davis was born in Birmingham, Alabama and grew up in Mobile. Her father was a minister in the deep South. As a result she became a committed Christian at the early age of twelve years.

"Mrs. Davis has been married for thirty eight years to Robert Davis. They have three children.

"Her ministry began at age of twenty two as a Christian counselor working with addicts from the street. She started an Alcoholic Anonymous as well as a Narcotics Anonymous program in the Needles Eye in Youngstown, Ohio.

"She has been honored and recognized by many organizations.She received The Good Samaritan Award from her community in 1984, was named Alcohol Administer of the Year in August 1987. One thousand dollars were given in her name to Third World countries for polio vaccine by the Paul Harris Fellow Award by the Rotary Foundation of Rotary International. This was enough vaccine to immunize eight million people at that time. The Iota Phi Lambda Sorority Incorporated honored her for business and professional community involvement on November 14, 1987. She was invited by Nancy Reagan to attend the 'Just Say No' program at the White House.

She is a certified alcohol counsellor in the State of Ohio. I am pleased to present Mrs. Irma Davis."

Mrs. Davis rose, looked at the audience and began: "Well, just relax. All of you sit there so straight! I praise the Lord for being here. Before I go into my speech I'd like to pray a minute.

"Lord, we want to thank you that you are God. And, Lord, we want to thank you that you love us right where we are. We ask that you would touch each ear so they may hear what the Spirit of the Lord is saying to your church today that as we leave this room today we would have a new challenge, and go out to bring the sheep that is lost into the kingdom. We ask this in your name. Amen."

This many-faceted woman, a natural-born story teller, stared at her audience; immediately they became quiet. Then she smiled her approval and from that moment held the audience spellbound as she painted verbal pictures. Her face reflected her mood. "I want to talk about the issues the black family is facing. Everybody (the news media, social services, people who don't understand) is criticizing the black family. They say, 'The black family don't know this, the black family don't do that.' Today I want to talk especially about black children and parenting.

Discrimination and racism brought changes to our family. It changed our value system. That's why we have so many problems. We had poor living conditions and poor housing after slavery. The disorganization of homes brought about some of the problems we still have."

Suddenly the listeners found themselves visualizing a little country church where the speaker's father not only taught Sunday school but with chalk in his hand stood at the blackboard ready to teach the black people their ABC's.

She said, "The black church was everything. Politics, how to have babies, what you gonna eat and how you gonna eat it.

"The whole value system of the black folks started in the church. Now it's changed. People are uppity. They do whatever feels good and forget about the power of God in their lives."

Next the audience was transported mentally to a little shack. "One of the biggest problems here is the absence of the father," she said. "The black woman tries to fill in the gap but it isn't the same. Where is the man who helped create these babies? He's out there having a good time. The woman is tied to the house. It is time that husbands return as fathers, leaders and providers."

Frowns appeared on faces of the listeners as they sensed

the truth of her statement.

Then, looking straight at the young men and with a pointed finger, she continued, "As Christians we need to teach that there should be no sex before marriage. As a church we need to teach that. If you can't be a father then don't make a baby!"

A whispered under-the-breath "Amen" was heard.

She compared the Christian life to a football huddle with the cheerleaders yelling:

The team is in a huddle
The captain raised his head
They all got together
And this is what they said,
Fight, team, fight!

Now she was speaking their language. They joined in.

Fight, team, fight!
Fight, team, fight team!
Fight, fight, fight!

"God is speaking to you to get out of the huddle if we are to help our people. A football team's no good only staying in a huddle. It needs to get out there and fight!"

After describing the Needle's Eye Women's Support Group, Mrs. Davis read statements from the ladies interviewed in a poll to find out what problems the black family is facing. She read a few of the comments.

"Black fathers are weak. They don't think. They are not listening and have forgotten about God," said a lady in her twenties..

"I am afraid of addicted people. I want to die!" said one, sixty eight.

"Government is at fault. Instead of jobs, they give us a little money and food stamps. We want to work. We need respect from the world. Everybody thinks we want to be on welfare and not work. I want a job!" said another not yet thirty.

In a casual, relaxed manner stories began to flow out of Irma Davis's own gut feelings about life. "We black folk are actors. In Rome I act like the Romans. I can say, 'Yes, sir!' I can look down my nose at you. (Her head was held high; snickers were heard.) I know the street language. They call me 'South

Side Mama.'"

Someone in the audience called out, "Hi, South Side Mama." Everyone grinned as she waved, smiled and continued.

"You don't have to be somebody else. You can be yourself. God made you the way he wanted you to be."

"Right on!" chanted the college voices.

"I had a heart attack and two strokes besides having cancer with chemotherapy. But God isn't finished with me yet. I won't die until He's ready for me! I still have work to do. I go into the Needle's Eye and listen to the six-year-old pray, 'Lord, help me in my trials and tribulations.'

"I see the seven-year-old alcoholic. I know he can change. God can change him. I see it happen all the time. We take the kids to movies, to the farm and show them a better way of life. I tell them to stand up, I say, "You got personality."

To this and many similar words the crowd responded. When she was finished speaking many refused to leave. Students rushed up, clung to her and begged her to be their mentor. "Help us get started," they begged. "We want to help."

"Here's my address. Write to me."

"When can we hear more from you?"

She started to her room but was followed by students begging for more. She tried to pull herself away but they clung to her and followed her to her hotel room. Graciously she invited them in and they sat and talked.

TABLE OF CONTENTS

Acknowledgements
Preface
Introduction

Chapter 1	"Crisis"	1
Chapter 2	"My Childhood"	9
Chapter 3	"Good News Club"	17
Chapter 4	"Walking Straight"	25
Chapter 5	"About the City"	33
Chapter 6	"Meet Irma Davis"	41
Chapter 7	"Meeting and Marrying"	47
Chapter 8	"Life in Youngstown"	53
Chapter 9	"The Needle's Eye"	61
Chapter 10	"What's Going On Here?"	67
Chapter 11	"Fireside Chat"	75
Chapter 12	"Twelve Steps"	83
Chapter 13	"Youth Work"	91
Chapter 14	""Models"	101

Epilogue

Chapter 1
"Crisis"

"Who's at the door at this hour of the night?" I asked my husband.
"I don't know, but I'll go see."
I did not recognize the voice of the young man to whom my husband was speaking. There was anxiety in the husky voice outside the door as he asked to come in. My husband opened the door, bade him welcome.
By then I had jumped up, grabbed my robe and hurried to the kitchen to take a look. The visitor was in his late teens, rather small-featured, shabbily dressed, hair rather long and stringy. He had a hacking cough.
"You . . . you don't remember me?" he asked nervously. "I used to come here when my friend Blake had your son Ethan to fix his car."
"Oh, yes, I do remember Blake had someone with him," Calvin said. "That was last summer, wasn't it?"
Thoughts were racing through my mind. What did he want? Was he to be trusted?
"And what is your name?" asked Calvin.

"I'm Alf. Alf Singer. I live between Canton and Youngstown," he said. I noticed that his breath was wheezy.

We seated ourselves by the kitchen table. He talked about Blakes's antique car, how it was running smoothly. He asked about our grandchildren. He remembered swinging them on the back lawn.

I said to myself, That's not why this young man came here. What does he really want?

We chatted a bit longer. We were silent for a while; then, as though he was mustering up courage, he twisted his cap nervously in his hands.

"I . . . I . . . got a problem and thought maybe you could help me."

Calvin encouraged him with a nod.

"I came here because you are the only Christians I know and I thought maybe you could help me."

Only Christian he knows? I repeated inwardly.

"The other night my girlfriend and I had a big fight. We broke up and I went home and took all kinds of drugs."

Drugs? I said to myself. He's on drugs? Already I projected we could not be much help to him.

He stopped to cough, then continued, "It wasn't a good idea. Soon after I took them I felt myself slipping downward."

There I was again, asking unanswerable questions: Is he saying he felt he was dying? Why was he going downward?

"Hot flames were licking at my feet and I was getting hotter and hotter.

"Suddenly I realized that I was dying and was on the way to hell!"

I caught Calvin's expression. This boy not only had one problem but a complexity of problems!

"I wasn't ready to die! I didn't want to die."

He fought back a tear and his coughing started again. I went to get a cup of water and placed it before him.

When his coughing subsided he continued. "I've heard there is a God in Heaven but I never talked to him before. But at that moment I was desperate. I cried out, "God up in Heaven, help me! Save me!'"

My husband's eyes widened. In all our years of experience we had never heard such a story! I clasped Calvin's hand under the table and gave it a hard squeeze.

Alf paused, then continued. "You know something? I really meant it. I promised God that if He'd save me, I'd do something to turn my life around."

"Did you do that?" I asked.

"That's why I'm here. I need help. But I want to finish my story. At that moment I felt a hand grab my hair and pull me back up. I knew it was God 'cause when I looked around there was no one in sight and I was back on earth and I wasn't dead. That's why I'm here. I want to know God. I want to get off drugs. Can you help me?"

Later Alf was sleeping in our spare bedroom upstairs. Calvin and I had cozied ourselves in our own bed. I breathed into his flannel pajamas and said, "Hon, what are we going to do to help Alf? We don't know anything about him except that he used to come along with Blake when Ethan worked on his car. How did he decide we were Christians?"

"Calm down, dear. It doesn't matter how he arrived at his decision. You heard what he said and know as much as I. He needs help and we will find a way to help him."

"Fine and good," I said as I sat up straight in bed. "And just what do you and I know about drug addiction? We don't know anything!"

He pulled me back into his arms. "But we can learn. Look at it this way. If the Lord led him here then we've got to try. Why don't we pray about it?"

The next morning as Alf pulled out of our drive in his rickety car, I clasped the paper on which he had written his name, address, and telephone number. Checking my watch, I was reminded that this was Saturday, that I had been in the classroom all week with 35 rambunctious fifth graders, that there was laundry piled high and lots of weekend chores to do, and that I had signed up for a weekend women's retreat at Pilgrim Hills. I dashed through necessities, gave my husband a quick kiss and was off.

When I arrived at the camp I registered, unloaded my suitcase and went to the dining room, where the women were waiting for the meeting to begin. I looked about the room and saw a middle-aged black lady sitting by herself.

"May I sit by you?" I inquired.

"I'm not saving it for anyone," she replied. We chatted a bit then she introduced herself.

"I'm Irma Davis and I'm in charge of the Needle's Eye in Youngstown, Ohio."

"Needle's Eye? Tell me, what's that?"

"You know the story in the Bible where Jesus said it was easier for a camel to squeeze through the eye of a needle than for some persons to change their lifestyle to conform to the standard of his kingdom?"

"Yes, go on."

"Well, the Needle's Eye is a Christian counselling center for drug addicts and alcohol abusers."

The electrons were connecting with the protons! I was getting a connection one could call an instant friendship.

Leaning forward I gasped, "You know how to help drug addicts?"

"That's my job."

I knew it <u>didn't just happen</u>. The moment I got home Sunday night I told Calvin about the Needle's Eye and that we had an appointment to take Alf there first thing in the morning.

"But you're teaching and . . ."

"I'll call work and take a personal leave."

Connections were made and soon Calvin and I, with Alf in the back seat, were rolling down Hillman Street in Youngstown towards the Needle's Eye in the toughest part of town.

We all looked for the building. Alf spied it first. "Look. There's a picture of a big needle with a thread running through it. It's got to be the Needle's Eye!" he said.

We parked in front of the building, which resembled a cracker box with a huge glass window in the front. The glass was

boarded up inside so one couldn't be sure what was behind it.
"Howdy. I've been waiting for you," called out Irma Davis. She offered us coffee the moment we entered; then, like a mother hen sheltering her chicks, she focused her attention on Alf.
"Tell me about yourself. Did you eat breakfast? Tell me about your family . . ."
As she talked to him I looked about the small reception room. It had a large desk with a wooden chair pushed under it, a few rusty folding chairs. There wasn't much else. Through a doorway I could see a much larger uncarpeted floor, which creaked as a woman walked over it bringing us some coffee. The dimly lit room, due to the boarded-up glass front, had only a small light bulb hanging from the ceiling.
I noticed people coming in and joining the group. They dropped in one at a time and casually formed a circle around us.
"Who are these people and where is everyone coming from?" I whispered to the one nearest me.
"We're the counsellors. In this system we drop anything we're doing when the call comes and we rush over." Soon there were eight people in the circle and they were starting to pray. The founder of the Needle's Eye broke into a fervent prayer with hands and face raised heavenward.
"Lord Jesus, help Alf Singer. You have the power to take away from him all desire for drugs. You long to have him for your very own. Right now we ask you to fill him with your love. Help him to be strong and to say no to drugs. Save him, Lord..."
Everyone placed their hands on Alf. He closed his eyes, then in a faltering voice began to pray, "I want to know you, Father. I want to be your servant as I promised you."
When the last "amens" and "hallelujahs" were said, Irma looked straight into his eyes. "Alf, you told me you were smoking marijuana, then you took heroine and a dellida. This combination of synthetics is a killer. How is it you're not dead?"
Tears spilled down his cheeks as he repeated the harassing experience of slipping into hell. The counsellors looked on in silent amazement, then all spoke at once.
"You are lucky to be alive, Alf."

"God spared your life."
"Can you believe it?"
"Amazing!"

Then Mrs. Davis pulled him to his feet. "You've made a new start today, Alf. But this is only the beginning of your new life. What you need to do is join one of the rehabilitation programs we have available. "I'm hoping to enroll you in a program that uses the gospel approach. There are others but in this one you will study the Bible along with a work program. It will make it easier than trying to grow spiritually on your own."

He nodded and I knew we were on the right trail.

"Is this her procedure for everyone who comes here?" I asked a counsellor.

"Oh, no! It depends on the need. There is a basic form Mrs. Davis fills in for everybody. She finds out by counselling them exactly what their need is and goes from there. If she senses that there is a financial need she may refer them to the welfare office, or if they need food, we have some groceries we can give them. Each case is different."

"Ah, ha. She sensed Alf's spiritual need and that is the reason for this response," I concluded.

When Irma heard Alf express interest in the program she described to him, she left to call the Teen Challenge at Pataskala and returned shortly with a smile on her face.

"The Lord must want you there. There is one bed unoccupied. They'll take you today. Are you free to go?" she asked Alf.

"Yes, I'll go," he answered quickly.

We made arrangements to get Alf's clothing, stop back to pick up Mrs. Davis and her husband and together take him to Pataskala. Calvin and I, along with Alf, hopped in the car and drove to his home. When we arrived, Alf motioned for us to follow him into the house.

"Hi, Mom, I'm home," he yelled as he entered but his mother didn't seem to notice. She was sitting in the living room amid a blaring television and three bawling grandchildren. She and the grandchildren did not seem to relate well to one another. It was not the constant reprimanding in a high shrill voice that bothered me as much as her neglect. She had ignored Alf; she had paid no attention to us when we entered. We moved closer to the living room as Alf ran upstairs. When she couldn't help but notice us, she pointed to the chairs in front of the television as if to suggest we watch it with her.

At the first commercial break we introduced ourselves and tried to explain our presence. "We're friends of your son and have come to get Alf's clothes and take him to a rehabilitation center."

Mrs. Singer shrugged her shoulders and kept yelling at the children's slightest misbehavior.

Soon Alf appeared coming down the stairs with a suitcase. She raised no questions; neither did she say goodbye, so we left.

"Doesn't she mind if you go?" I asked curiously.

"Naw, she doesn't care what happens to me," he said gruffly.

We picked up the Davises, squeezed ourselves into our small compact car, and started on our three-hour trip. They had been to the teen center before and knew where to find it. When we arrived we were soon convinced that it was the right place for Alf Singer. Here he would get medical treatment, have Christian counselling, and it would be a place where he could grow in his new-found faith in God.

As the Davises and we started on our trip home, I was happy for the time we would have riding together. It would give me a chance to learn to know Irma Davis, a lady who seemed to have so little but demanded so much respect.

The time was too short. We laughed, talked, and shared. I was convinced that I had only begun touching the riches Irma had to offer. In those three hours she captivated us with the stories of her early childhood.

Chapter 2
"My Childhood"

I, Irma Nell Washington Davis, was born in the hallway of the Jefferson Hospital in Birmingham, Alabama, before they got my mother to the delivery room. The nurse yelled, "Your husband ought to be here to clean up the mess!" It was the day after Christmas in 1930. We lived there about two years then moved to Gulfport.

My father was the pastor at the Apostolic Church, and the bishop of the Apostolic Overcoming Holiness Church of God for all of Alabama, Mississippi and southern Louisiana. He was a tall man, six feet one inch tall. Everybody liked him and he liked everybody. It was his nature to be talkative; what he said made sense for he had been well educated at the Wilburforce College in Ohio. The church sent him South to Mobile to run a revival. He'd preach under the chinaberry trees or hold brush arbor meetings. Brush arbor was a make-shift tent, made out of brush stacked over some sticks to provide shade for the people who came far and wide to hear my father preach.

My mother was part Black Creek Indian. She was only four feet nine inches tall with high cheek bones. She was a soft-spoken woman who seemed shy, but she wasn't really. My mother did whatever Dad said she should, without raising a fuss.

My father met my mother when he stayed at the preacher's home. Bishop W.T. Phillips kept his hired girl as an extended member of the family. That was my mother.

My father, David Washington, fell in love and married Millie Lee Allen. They had three children before I came along. The oldest boy they called David; next came James Lee, Sadie Elizabeth, and then me, Irma Nell. I was the last but later they kept a girl named Melba whose mother had passed away. She came to live with us.

My father traveled a lot. He came home weekends, but my mother was the one who taught us according to the scripture. She did everything according to the Bible. Because Abraham's wife Sarah of Old Testament times called her husband "My Lord," my mother called my father by the same title of respect.

My family was of very strict "Hook-and-Eye-Pentecostal" background, so they were very, very tough on us. The clothes we wore were black, dark blue, grey, white or beige. We were never allowed to say OK or cross our legs. That was a sin. We didn't eat pork, didn't drink coffee. We could eat chocolate cake but we could never call it devil's food cake. We went to church every Sunday all day and went back to the night services.

My father was a man of faith. Lots of times we kids would feel ashamed of all this faith stuff. When my father would go to the train station he'd walk up to a white man who would greet him, saying, "Hi, Reverend, how are you?"

"Yes, sir, I'm fine."

"Now what do you want?" the man would say.

"I want a round-trip ticket to Gulfport, Mississippi. I'll pay you when I get back. These tickets will be for four children, mother and myself." My father went by faith that the man would give him the tickets.

If we got the tickets we could go with him. Whenever we were going, the folks there would take the collection, then my dad would pay for the ride. Sometimes there might be a dollar left over. The church people would take a pound collection. They'd give us things such as a pound of rice, beans, jelly, potatoes, fish, and lard and we'd live on that.

We'd go on to Vinegar Bend, Alabama, where we'd sing and father would preach. Vinegar Bend is a farm with pine trees. Little cups hung on the trees which would catch the sap called quim, which was made into turpentine.

The people at that place lived as if they were still in slavery. They could not read or write, and a white man owned the farm and shacks. Those people were always in debt. There was an electric wire fence all around the farm. The white man would tell them that if they left they had to pay up, or else he would take one of their children, always a son whom he'd keep to work.

So the people stayed.

My father would go in and out of the various farms where the black people lived and preach to them. Most places they had a little church on the farm, so that's where they'd meet. They liked my father for he was educated and knew what to say to them. He'd preach, and when he'd come up to the owner the white man would say, "Cook good for the preacher."

My father didn't eat meat, only greens and fish, and they had a lot of that. They'd have everything to eat when he came.

Each time he left a place he would smuggle a person out with him. He would hide someone in the trunk of the car under all the greens, potatoes, chicken and rabbits the people gave him instead of pay.

When the people were missed the white man would put the dogs out after them, but the dogs couldn't find them. My father would always go by the river and get the car wet so the dogs couldn't get the scent.

They never suspected my father. The people would cover up for him by talking of the hole in the fence or some other story to guide the white man off the track.

One time he almost got caught. He had just smuggled out a woman and her four children. A funeral director came to his aid by putting them in five coffins and shipping them over to Birmingham, Alabama, where they could catch the train and head towards Cleveland, Ohio. There they could get their freedom. The black folk would say, "I'm gonna' catch a forty going north."

This family who was shipped out in coffins, is now living a productive life in Cleveland and all of them are Christians.

My father believed he could do anything through Christ. We went everywhere on faith and God opened up doors for us. We traveled a lot all over the south. Sometimes we went west but we were poor. My father believed that God wanted him to get out the Word, and that God would provide for us wherever we went.

But many times we didn't have food. My mother would cook all she had. I would hear her praying at night: "God put me and these children on someone's heart. We are out of food."

The next day she would sit down at the table with a nice table cloth made from a feed sack, with beautiful napkins made from flour sacks. But we would sit and wait there in front of our nice tin plates and tin cups. She would say the blessing over the food that wasn't there. There was no food on the stove or the table, but before she was finished praying there would be a knock and we would run to see someone standing at the door.

"Mrs. Washington, here is a pot of soup," we might hear. Sometimes there were beans but always bread pudding or rice pudding. Everybody and everything--we, the dog, the cat--all had to fast. The dog and cat would go scratching at the ice box. Sometimes we would have a complete fast for three or four days. I always believed that some of those fasts were because we didn't have any food.

One thing we usually had a lot of was biscuits. My mother served us syrup and bread all the time until my sister and I got tired of the same thing.

One Sunday my father preached his sermon about "Casting Your Bread on the Water." He said, "If you do that, in many day hence it will come back to you." So we did just that. We went to the river and every day we'd come home late because we'd taken our lunch biscuits and put them on the river. Every day we'd go by to wait for a loaf of light bread to come back. That was the thing we wanted--to be able to eat light bread from the store. It never came and we got mad. One day my father caught us down on the river bank, waiting. He made us to understand what God's Word meant, so we got that straightened out.

You know, we got faith put into us while we were small; we were taught that God will make a way out of no way. One time my brother cut his foot really bad. We had no money for the doctor, so my father blessed it with oil, washed out the wound with lye soap and prayed over it. It was all right.

We had a wood-burning stove, an outside toilet, and had to carry water. We called it toting water. We also didn't have electric lights. We had oil lamps instead. We kept the shades very clean and sparkling by washing them in lye soap.

Later we did get a phone and an inside bathroom. How grateful I was that I didn't have to go outside to the toilet anymore. But then, my father got up in church and made an announcement: He said, "We have a bathroom. You may come and take a bath." How I hated it! The church folk came to bathe on Saturday.

I remember the time I saw my first pretty soap. It was pink and was called sweet soap. I tasted it to see if it was really sweet.

Because I was big for my age, they always expected me to do everything. I always had to help make soap in the big black pot outside and to carry water down the hill to wash. The school was about six miles away, so we had to get up early and wash clothes before we went to school. If we didn't wash them clean my mother would take them off the line and throw them on the ground. We had to wash them all over again.

My father didn't wear anything but white shirts. We had to iron sometimes for an hour without stopping. We cleaned his hat with corn meal and cleaned his suit with gas. We went down to the store and got a nickel's worth of gas to clean my father's suit, and then we'd hang it out to air. We were taught to work with strict discipline.

It was not unusual for me to cut wood like a boy. We all had to tote ice about half a mile for our ice box. We had to run all the way back so it would not melt.

God always provided for us. I remember one Sunday we went to prison with my father, who preached there. On our way back from Atmore Prison, we stopped at the church for the night service. On our way to Atmore our car had a flat tire and we had no spare. (Back then the cars did not have all those extras.) So there we were in a hick town, black, and with no tire. My father started to pray, my mother got out her Bible, then along came the sheriff. (Sheriffs were always fat and loud.) He said, "What's wrong now?"

My father said, "I am Reverend Washington from Mobile, Alabama. We were singing and praying here having church under this chinaberry tree."

"Hush all this singing and praying," the sheriff said. "It's not going to get you niggers anywhere. That's all you niggers think about-Him.' With this he pointed up in heaven.

We started to tap the tambourine and sing. The Lord moved him with compassion. He came back and brought us a used tire.

My father was never afraid to ask or pray out loud. He wanted everybody to know what side he was on.

I always went with my father to sing at the revival. I had to sing before he preached. I loved that. I came to know Jesus in a personal way when I was twelve years old.

I was a devilish kid but maybe God was getting me ready for the ministry I am now in. Once when I was about thirteen I decided to have church after our choir rehearsal. We had our own service just like my father's. I had a tea party and served communion at the same time. I served the juice and the bread just like my father did. We ate all that was in the church.

Come next Sunday, there was no juice, nor bread, in the service. My father stood up and said, "Irma Nell, come up here. Where is the communion?"

"Well, well . . . I had communion Friday after choir practice."

My father looked me straight in the eye and said, "Well, you just come up here." He put me on the altar and all the while the church service went on and I had to pray out loud and confess my sins.

He preached about forty-five minutes while I was on my knees praying. I was very sorry but I still thought what I'd done was OK. He never called the other kids up. It was always me, all the time. He knew that I was the leader and that the rest would follow me.

Some people said the preachers' children were awful. I'd thought I was doing something good. Well, I got a whipping for serving the communion, but even then I knew God was going to use me. I didn't know in what. They all called me "Big Nell" cause I was big and tall, and they believed I could work hard and do everything. Whatever I said we were going to do, we did it.

Our choir was the Allenville Gospel Choir. Allenville was a seaport town close to Mobile, a nice place to live. There were about sixteen girls and two boys in the choir. We had one guy who was really a gifted piano player. Everywhere my father went to preach, we went to sing. Our choir was the first black choir ever to be on the radio every Sunday morning at 7:30.

We'd sing what blacks and whites wanted us to sing. Our theme song was "Touch Me, Lord Jesus." We became famous in our town and county because God blessed us. We were asked to be on a program one time with Rosetta Tharpe, a great singer. Another time, we appeared on a program with the five blind boys of Mississippi. We were always called upon to sing.

The Lord truly was in us. Even in the foolish things we did. He understood us.

My father would say, "They are children and they must act like children." He believed in discipline, but he loved us and understood.

Chapter 3
"Good News Club"

It was late afternoon by the time Calvin and I dropped the Davises off in Youngstown. As I looked at the Needle's Eye, I turned to Irma and said, "I have the feeling that there is alot going on in there that I don't know about."

"You're probably right," she replied. Then, as though a light had gone on, she said, "You work with children. Why don't you come down Saturday in two weeks and see what we do in the Good News Club? We help people like Alf, all right, but my whole emphasis is on prevention rather than cure. You really need to see our children's program."

It could give me some ideas for my own classroom, I thought. As we parted company I promised to return.

When Calvin and I arrived to the Needle's Eye on Saturday morning a few weeks later, Irma Davis welcomed us with a beaming smile. "I'm glad you came early. Now I can tell you a bit about the Good News Club before the children arrive," she said.

She went to pour us a cup of coffee, giving us a moment to look about. The rectangular wooden building was divided into two rooms. The front room, dimly lit, had a desk and a few folding chairs. The walls were filled with photos of the young people's activities, hand-printed posters entitled "Ten Commandments for Teen-agers," "A Pledge for African People," "Human Values," "Ten Commandments for Parents," "Pep Talk for Students," "Pledge to Stay Drug-Free," and many other drug-related posters.

The large backroom was anything but plush. It had lots of floor space, a piano, some metal chairs, a large ping-pong table and a small library with magazines and some songbooks.

"The Good News Club meets every Saturday morning," she said when she returned. "There are about forty who attend, sometimes more. These kids come from broken or addicted homes. Just last week I saw a girl who was so tired. I said to her, 'Why are you so tired?'

"It wasn't my turn to sleep last night," she said.

"What you mean?" I asked, "It wasn't my turn to sleep?"

"There aren't any extra blankets and just one bed for everybody and we take turns," she answered. "It wasn't my turn last night."

"You believed her?" I asked.

"Sure did. A lot of kids who come here just don't have anything. It's their way of life. We try to find out what their needs are and then try to help them. I feel sorry for abused children. You can pick them out. They're skinny, often have scars on their bodies, and look scared. Abused kids are sent to our program from Children Services. We believe that if we get children in our program by the time they are five, and if we get the gospel into them and discipline into them, they will make it."

"It looks like a challenge. You seem busy," Calvin said.

"Yes, we are. We have young people in the program, aged five to twenty two. They like to come 'cause we have movies, we take them camping, and have recovering addicts who come and talk to them. We teach them the books of the Bible by 'rapping' the words to music. We use upbeat songs, and have rap music sessions and crafts. Just recently we formed a new group for adolescent girls to deal with problems of dating. There are things they need to know that didn't fit the needs of the whole group. We do that when necessary."

"It sounds like you meet the need with a program," I said.

"We try. We have kids' seminars just for kids. We have a lot of teaching on who we are. I believe that if you don't know where you come from you won't know where you're going. We want these kids to be proud of who they are. We take them to places like the college where my father attended at Wilbur Force, to the museum and to a site of the Underground Railroad. In November we have parade drill teams. We celebrate Alcoholic Month. So it's a big thing with the children. It works. We make buttons and sell them to make money for camp. We feed some kids every Saturday. About the fifteenth of the month they all are hungry because food has all run out at home."

"Who furnishes the food?" I asked her.

"Lots of the churches in the area take up special offerings. Some folks bring in things," she said. "Once we had a turkey for Thanksgiving. We fed two hundred people with that turkey. The turkey increased until everyone was fed."

Again my mind questioned her statement. One turkey feeding two hundred people? They must have only had a smidgen! Or could it possibly have been a miracle like the time Christ fed the 5,000 people? It was not in my realm of experience but I had no reason to doubt it.

The first children were beginning to arrive. They gathered around us and we chatted.

"What do you do in Good News Club?" I asked a small black boy with bright eyes.

"We sing."

Others quickly volunteered answers.

"We do puppets."

Sometimes Mrs. Davis tells us stories.

"I like the hot dogs. I can eat three!"

"We learn Bible verses."

More children kept coming in an orderly fashion. They sat around on the floor in a big circle. Sophia Brooks came to the piano and began singing with the children.

"She has a gorgeous voice," I whispered to Mrs. Davis.

"Oh, yes, she sings solos with the Youngstown Symphony. She is a volunteer who comes to work with the children each week. Sometimes she has the children's choir appear on her television program over channel twenty seven here in Youngstown."

"She has a show of her own?" I asked.

Mrs. Davis nodded her head. "It's a talk show. She's the emcee."

When Irma Davis once again took over she looked straight into the youngsters' eyes and said, "You are a good group of children. The world is waiting for you. God has so much waiting for you, it blows my mind!"

Then she turned to a young man who entered. "Look. Here is Herman! I get so excited about what God can do with a man. He was sick. We prayed for him and he is well! Let's give him a hand."

After everyone was comfortable she looked at the group and said, "Irma Davis likes to look at black folk. You are beautiful." The children turned to look at each other and smiled.

"Children," she said, "We have a special visitor who is going to speak to you. She came all the way from Warren. Her name is Delores Smith. I want you to pay very close attention. She has something worthwhile to say and you won't want to miss it."

All eyes focused on an attractive black woman who stood tall. She smiled, chatted a bit, then started with a question.

"Did you ever watch Tarzan on television? Did you notice that Tarzan always comes through the trees to black people who mumble? That's not a true image of Africa! I came to tell you that there are a lot of untrue stories about black people. Today we want to learn the truth about us black folks.

"Alkebu-lan is the original name of Africa and the name means 'Motherland.' Alkebu-lan is the home of black culture that started in Ethiopia, a land so beautiful that it is often referred to as the Garden of Eden. It has sturdy forests, artistic gardens and orderly civilization. The land was once ruled by Solomon along with his most respected Nubian queen Sheba.

"Nubian" is a name given to black folk. The Nubians were and still are the predominant race in Africa. They first lived by the Upper Nile River as farmers. The people were known for their caravans, and just like you children today, they were curious to see what else they could find in the world; so they went to see. They followed the rivers and cultivated the lands wherever they went. Once in Egypt, all citizens became Egyptians. Most of the Egyptians were Nubians.

"If you knew how brilliant your ancestors were, you wouldn't feel like you can't learn. Does anyone here know some of the contributions black people have given the world?"

One voice ventured a guess. "Jewelry?"

Another, "Medicine?"

Mrs. Smith smiled, then continued. "I'll name a few for you.One is the first calendar that we still use today, another is the ancient pyramids that were built by one of our ancestors, a very dark Nubian, by the name of Imhotep of Egypt. This chief architect was a multi-genius. He was known as 'The God of Medicine,' so the person who said 'medicine' guessed correctly. He was the world's first doctor and performed the first heart and first brain surgery. Today they still use the oath he wrote.

"Another man, named Dartus I, founded and introduced the system of 'money exchange.' Did you ever hear someone say, 'Charge it'? That credit system was started by black king Mansa Moussa.

"Why do I want you to know this? Someone told me that I couldn't do math. Do you know what I thought? If our ancestors gave the world mathematics I can do math.There's no excuse for us believing we can't learn. Our ancestors were brilliant. How else could they build the pyramids, and start the credit system and money exchange?

"Scientists didn't give credit to the Nubians for that. The world forgets to tell you it was your ancestors who gave you the royal system of civil service, and started agricultural trade. They don't tell you we gave scholarships to their bright youth and sent them to university.

"Back then men were put in universities for forty years. They had no contact with females. Just think you'd be in school from age seven to forty-seven.

"Some children today holler and scream 'cause you're asked to be in school twelve to sixteen years. Then school wasn't for women. Today girls can go to school. You ought to take full advantage and stay in school. It's a privilege.

"You sometimes hear some myths about Africa. Do you know any?"

It kept Mrs. Smith busy pointing to children with hands raised.

"Jungles."

"Slave women."

"They're jet black and greasy."

"They walk with bones through their noses!"

"Cannibals and savages."

"They are ignorant and eat their children."

"Everybody is poor . . ."

The speaker looked surprised, then she asked, "Do you believe these myths?"

The children shook their heads and shouted, "No!"

She went on. "If that's all you knew about Africa, would you want to belong to it? It would make you feel ashamed.

"Africa hasn't always been poor. Did you know that ninety percent of the diamonds, eighty five percent of the gold and twenty five percent of the coffee comes out of Africa? People take all these things out and don't put anything back in. "Myths are told to make you feel ashamed. Don't believe all you hear. Our people were not pagan. They were a religious people and believed in one God. The oldest Christian nation in the world is Ethiopia. They developed the education, political and family systems. These are all valuable.

"Our women developed hair styles we call corn rows or dread locks. We gave the world music to dance to drums, and rhythms that were retained from Africa and are still being used here in America today."

The children's attention focused on the speaker as she continued, "White people wanted to carve Africa into small pieces. Everyone took pieces of the continent. White people stole

Needle's Eye Page 23

the Africans in slave trade and brought them to America. Why do you think they wanted to scoop them up by the million if they had no value? You know what they called us? 'Black Gold' or 'Black Ivory.' They knew we had skills in agriculture, irrigation, architecture, navigation and metallurgy and these things were high in demand when the European nations began their exploration of other portions of the world. They stole our men, women, children and even the elderly and shipped them to America because we Nubians knew how to build the farms and plantation as and cities.

"Some black folk were dropped off in Haiti and were bred like animals. The white people took the babies from the mothers' breasts and programmed them to be folks of a lost culture, which made them feel valueless, and turned them into workhorses. You are programmed to think you are of no value. It's not true!

"Blacks were to be held in bondage for a lifetime. Some fought against being in slavery. Some tried to run away, but do you think they succeeded? No. The color of their skin didn't let them hide. It was like being a fly in buttermilk. It doesn't let you hide.

"The white folk were determined that blacks should never be free. They chopped off their legs, or hanged them when they tried to escape. But our people taught themselves to read and write.

"Harriet Tubman hated slavery. She determined to let people be free. She helped three hundred black folk to freedom. She used Negro spirituals for signals. If they sang 'Steal Away' that meant they were to drop everything and travel by night.

"If they sang 'Wade in the Water' that meant they'd walk through the water so dogs couldn't follow their scent. If there wasn't water close by they'd put pepper on the ground to cover the smell. Sometimes children carried a doll a certain way; it meant they needed a place to stay.

"Some white folk who hated slavery helped hide the slaves. Behind a shelf in the house they would have a big room where blacks could hide. They helped the black people on a journey that ended in Canada. Once the Civil War was over the black people came back to the United States.

"Nobody likes being a slave. But today many are still enslaved by an even worse enemy. There are four ways you are kept in slavery--if you use alcohol or drugs, get pregnant as a teen-ager, do not get educated, or--the worst one of all--if you lack cultural pride; then you are in slavery worse than our ancestors were. There is no way out unless you help yourself.

"Don't let someone else control your mind. You must think good about yourself and you must love God. True freedom is to think free! There is so much beauty in you. You gave the world so much. What you are and where you go depends on how you think."

As Delores Smith had finished speaking, Mrs. Davis said to the children, "Some of you will become Congress persons. Some of you will become good mothers and fathers. You have the best. This is the best Good News Club in America. Do you know why? We teach you about Jesus Christ.

"Now we're going to have refreshments. Let's repeat our slogan: 'Party with me. I'm drug free.'"

All the children chanted, "Party with me. I'm drug free," as they got in line in the polite way Mrs. Davis required.

Later, after the children and Mrs. Smith had gone, Mrs. Davis invited Calvin and me to her house a few blocks from the Needle's Eye. After a few minutes' drive we pulled in the narrow driveway banked on one side with a stone wall. Poppy stems without tops jutted out above it.

"What happened to the poppy tops?" I inquired. "Did you gather them for seed?"

"Interesting you noticed," said Irma. "I'm suspecting someone helped themselves to get a high. The poppies act like a drug. I'll have to replace poppies with some other flowers."

When we were comfortably seated I urged her to tell me more of her life. "Tell me about your teen-aged years," I begged.

Chapter 4
"Walking Straight"

When I got to be a teen-ager, I was very mischievous! I remember one lady who repeated everything she saw and heard. And she'd make up stories or just plain lie about us. She told my mother and father that coming home from school we had beaten up on her son. She told them that she had spoken to us and that we had talked back to her.

I promised myself I'd get even with her. My brother and I went into her chicken house and took a wheelbarrow full of manure, and dumped it in front of her steps on Easter Sunday, when they were dressed to death. They had to move all that "poopie" in order to get out the door. My brother James and I laughed till we cracked up.

One day on the street an older teen-ager attempted to rape me. He thought he could have any black girl he wanted, so he tried me out. I didn't know anything about karate, but now that I think about it, I used my weight and height and beat him up terribly. The police came to our house after I told my father what had happened. My father prayed about it and then he called the governor, Big Jim Forson. He came to our rescue.

My father made friends with all the people in high places. That was possible because he was a northerner and adjusted to their laws, so God blessed him in that way.

I remember the hangings, and how our people were hung up on "do-right" poles and flogged until they promised to "do-right." Sometimes those mean white people beat the ones strung up on poles so hard they died. All of us black folk were forced to go and see the hangings. I remember the time the sheriff looked up and saw my father. He said with a sneer, "Start praying, pastor." My father would pray out loud. I thought it was cold blooded! We kids weren't allowed to cry or say anything, but inside we wanted to get even. We'd sneak over and blow up the white man's chickens with an air pump or let his pigs out of their pen. I remember a family of white people whose son had tuberculosis, and that was a feared disease. The people wanted to kill all the T.B. germs in town so they decided to burn the house down.

God told my father early that morning to have those people moved. He went to them and suggested they go to another town. They listened to him and left. At midnight members of the Ku Klux Klan came riding on horses, carrying torches. They poured gasoline on the house and burned it to the ground. The church came together to help these people. They had a pound shower, brought blankets and things for them. My father took the things to the family.

Another time we had a lot of storms down there on the coast. We lived in a ragged house that had no glass windows. We had a wooden window, which you opened in the daytime by tying it up on a nail with a string. There were no screens. When it rained I thought there was more water inside than outside.

We'd wake up and have to move out because our house was full of water and the rats were swimming around us. One time I got bitten by a rat. My brother James and my father prayed over me and I was all right.

A great storm came through in 1946. We were warned to get out but we had no place to go so we stayed there. When the storm got right over our house my father went on the porch, raised his hands and said, "Lord, we are in your hands. Take care of us." That storm lifted right up and dropped in another little town.

We had a lot of company. Always someone stayed overnight or ate with us. When I was a kid they didn't call people "homeless"; they were called hobos. My father and mother would bring in the hobos and feed them and give them a bed in the church.

One time my father had a church in New Orleans, Louisiana. He was tough on his people who were into cults, and voodoo, and who scared away the French with their doings. My father, known as Bishop Washington, got up in the pulpit and said, "I am not scared of your roots, your voodoo, or anything you have. I have the Lord and you better not try anything."

The people got mad and fired him. It was May when they took back the church, and the house we lived in. They gave us some pots and pans and we went to the Mississippi River and stayed there all summer long. As a teenager I did not realize that we didn't have any place to stay. I thought we were on a picnic. We ate fish, we went fishing and swimming and we had fun, fun, and more fun. I did not realize we hadn't had a place to live until I was fifty years old. I learned about it one day when I told my brother who lived in Connecticut that we ought to go home together."

"What do you want to do?" he asked.

"Go to Louisiana where we lived when we were twelve years old," I answered.

"You fool," he said. "You don't want to go there. We didn't have no place to live."

I got mad. "What do you mean we didn't have no place to live? I'm going to ask our mother."

I did ask my mother and she said,"That's right. We lived on the bank of the river."

I said, "What is wrong with you all to let us go through that?"

"You had such a good time," she said. "You didn't even

know you went camping out. We had sheets and quilts and we slept under the stars. It was great, so why make a fuss?"

Every year on New Year's, my father would have revival. He invited Bishop James to come and preach for about three or four months in a row. Bishop James could really preach but it was too long. I don't care what he preached about; he would end his sermon like this: "If Gabriel would blow his trumpet tonight, who will be ready to go?"

The saints got fired up and they'd say, "I'll be ready to go." He'd get all the young people up at the altar praying.

We kids got together and said, "Let's fix him. He says the same thing every night. We are sick of this, so let's fix him." We did, and this is how we did it.

All the preachers wore black suits with a long coat and a tie. It was March and the wind would blow and blow. The church had no ceiling, only a bell tower in it. There was a night latch on the door.

That night one of the boys who had a horn crawled up in the bell tower and waited. We arranged that when the preacher got to saying, "If Gabriel blew his trumpet today, who would be ready to go?" we'd give him the signal to start blowing his horn.

The signal was given and the horn went, "TOO, TOO, DOO!" Then a surprising thing happened. The preacher picked up his Bible, jumped from the rostrum and started running out of the church. But he got caught. His coat tail was pinched in the door latch! He screamed, "Turn me loose, Gabriel. I'm not ready to go!"

We kids laughed and laughed and couldn't stop. My father punished us for it later but he laughed about it, just he and I. He would say, "Girl, you got a mind. Whoever would think up all of this foolishness?' Then he'd add, "You are a mess and you're not no mess of greens!" I understood my father and he understood me. A mess of greens to the black folks means you go to the garden to get the greens, you get only enough for just your family. The joke was just between him and me.

One of our neighbors had ten children. We were like brothers and sisters. One son was nicknamed "Mint." He wasn't scared of any thing and neither was I. We had a pet alligator we shared. We named the alligator Joey and loved his beautiful green color. We fed him well and he didn't stay a baby very long. He ate everything and anything from beans to fish to cornbread. The folks in the city complained to my father to do away with his kids' very large pet.

'Cause my father was away so much he had not seen Joey in a long time. But when more complaints came in he made us promise to get rid of Joey.

I ran to Mint's class to tell him what my father had said. My father decided to take him down to the ditch and then on Saturday take him to the Tinsaw River.

Mint and I had other plans. We had a new church and a pool of baptizing, so we put him in there. We had planned to get up before Sunday school and go get him out. Somehow we forgot. Come Sunday, the Baptist minister was preaching at our church. The Baptists always gave an invitation for members in the church to sing on their feet. They were singing "Take Me to the Water," just as Joey decided to start flopping around. The visiting preacher looked into the pool to see what was causing the ripples, and when he saw an alligator he took off running.

Well, the first person to get it was Irma Nell. My father called me up front, "Nell, you take that creature down to the river right now!" Mint and I and our friends caught that alligator and carried him down to the Tinsaw River and let him go. We didn't have any choice, but as it turned out the old folks went with us. After church we all got together in fellowship. We were all together, one in the Lord. You know, I miss those times.

My family used to go to Jackson, Alabama. That's a hicktown where blacks had a hard time. It was bad. We would go up there to sing and when one of us or all of us would go into the store, the store owner would try to make us do a dance before we could come out. Then we would tap dance, or sing, or act a fool so we'd be allowed to leave their store. The men would kick the owner in his behind. This was our signal that we were free to go.

When we told my father, he had a serious look on his face.

He said, "You are not a monkey. You are not to dance or sing for them. Do only what God tells you, not what the white crackers say."

When summer came the family would go with my father to Laurel, Mississippi, for the summer months. We ate snap beans, little white Irish potatoes and coarse ground yellow meal. We had that three times a day. We complained, "Can't we have something else for a change?"

"This is what God provided for you," my mother said. "Eat it."

When I got to be fourteen, I was bigger than all the kids around me, even the boys. I wore size twelve shoes. I hated my size so I walked bent over.

One day a lady from up North in Philadelphia came to our neighborhood. We thought she knew everything. She was a nurse, so if anyone got sick they would call her.

One time she hit me in my back and said, "Now you walk straight and I mean it." She smoked, and I thought she was just great. I thought any woman who was a nurse and smoked was great. So she talked to me and started me walking tall. She said, "I don't have what you folks have, but you are going to be something for God."

I kept that in mind. I didn't feel ugly any more, because she made me believe that I was special and had personality.

When I was in high school we heard some bad rumors about the preacher and the principal of our school. We girls got together and said we were going to make some money. We would get together and in our own handwriting copy all this news about people in our town, both good and bad. We called our paper "Brotherhood I."

We did pretty well selling those papers for three cents a piece until one of the teachers got hold of one and called my father who came to the school, and that was the end of "Brotherhood I." It seems my mind was always working on getting things going. We had our national meeting every year the first of June for ten days and nights. We were always trying to raise money to getting new clothes. This time we needed white dresses. We didn't get the money so my mother took the lace curtains at the window and made dresses out of it. Sadie and I were sharp.We took crepe paper and dyed some red ribbons.

My mother could really sew. She made coats out of old clothes, so we always looked good. She even made underwear and underskirts.They were always white; we were taught that all underclothing should be white if they were next to your skin.

Mother also could cook! She'd make sweet potato pies, lemon pies, and all kinds of things. We'd sell them at the wharf where the fishing boats came in. That way we would have money to buy food and clothing.

I went to Chicago one summer. It was great 'cause I heard all kinds of new things. There were unmarried girls having babies and girls who cursed or who cut their hair. They wore things I had never seen before. It seemed like heaven to me.

My father learned about this and lectured me. "Don't you have anything to do with those people!"

I couldn't understand it. I thought I had something to offer them, and I wanted to be with them. I knew God loved those people and had given me compassion for them. I understand now that my father was looking out for me. But I knew who I was in Christ then, and felt if you know who you are you can surely make it.

Chapter 5
"About the City"

"You want to see the city?" asked my hostess. "Hop in the car. I'll take you to the rehab centers."

I hopped in the front seat beside Irma Davis and we were off. We had barely started when my driver, a black woman in her early 60's, suddenly slowed down, leaned out the window and yelled at a child. "Missy, you get on home. Go find your mommy!"

I must have looked surprised, for she explained her action. "It's really not safe to have the children roaming the streets by themselves. Why the mother allows it, I don't know."

We drove by the skeletons of what had once been the sheet and tube buildings. My driver offered an explanation. "A few years ago Youngstown was the steel center in the country, and now look at it!"

I saw broken windows, sagging roofs and jagged steel structures standing as ghostly reminders that this had once been the industrial center where men earned weekly paychecks.

"What a shame!" I exclaimed. "How do people earn a

living?"

She continued. "People used to have respectable jobs. Now the main industry is drugs."

"Drugs? An industry?

"There's money in drugs. That's what keeps the business going. A drug pusher on the street can earn as much as $1,000 a week. That's big money and he uses it to buy a snazzy car."

I began to notice the cars on the street. "There's a Cadillac! Over there's a Saab, a Maeseratti, and even a Mercedes-Benz! I don't believe it!" I gasped.

I turned to Irma. "OK, you've convinced me. Drug pushers have money; but where do the people who have no jobs and are drug users get their money?"

"The need to support their habit is so intense they'll do anything to get money to buy drugs. They'll even sell the baby's clothes to get cocaine. Drugs become more important than food or sex. The greatest desire is to get drugs. The second- greatest desire is to get more drugs. Nothing else matters. Any money they get goes for drugs."

We drove by the housing project. It seemed each rectangular wooden building was built after the same stereotype blueprint. Scores of them stood row upon row. Trash lay on the street, in the gutter and around the grimy doorways.

"Jesse Jackson came from a housing project such as this. He did well; it's no disgrace where someone lives," said Mrs. Davis.

"It's a wonder what can come out of a ghetto. We come to pick up youth from this project for Bible school and the Good News Club. Sometimes there are two or three and sometimes as many as twenty come."

We turned around and bumped over the pot-holed road and were soon back at the main thoroughfare. On the corner of the intersection we noticed a young woman beckoning to a man in a passing car. My driver tooted the horn. The woman turned to look and cried out, "Ms. Davis! So good to see ya!" She ran over to meet us at the corner; Irma opened her car door, and the woman jumped into the back seat. It all happened before the light changed!

"Where might ye be goin'?" asked Mrs. Davis.
"I'm lost. Just tryin' to find my way around."
"Where ya be yesterday? I missed ya." (I was amazed at Mrs. Davis' ability to change her language mode so quickly to identify with the woman, who appeared to be in her late teens.)
"I couldn't fin' my way," she said with a glint in her eye.
"Mercie, ya always find it before. Listen to me, Mercie, I'm tryin' to find a place for your two babies so you can get 'em back. Now listen to me, young woman. You got to get your act together or you'll turn out like the other woman I know who is doin' just like you. She stopped comin' to the meetin's and soon she was right back on the street. That's what's gonna happen to you unless you stick with it!"

Mercie muttered some excuse about being hungry and having to go out to find something to eat.

"We give out food, Mercie. You know that. You didn't ask for food."

"I want meat."

"You want meat!" Mrs. Davis' voice was firm but kind.

By now we were at the rehabilitation center. It was a huge brick building with Victorian trim in the setting of trees and flowers.

"This is the rehab place," explained Mrs. Davis.

"I was here for three months," said Mercie.

"What happens at the rehab place?" I asked her.

"We live together, a bunch of women. We have counsellors and we go to lots of meetings," Mercie answered, rather unenthusiastically.

Mrs. Davis explained that it is the first place people on drugs are sent to learn to live without drugs and to become sober. "They get one-to-one counselling sessions by trained psychiatrists and are taken to the detoxification center for medical and physical treatment. There they learn about themselves, how to make themselves useful.

"I didn't like it here," said our rider.

"Why not?" I asked.

"They tell ya what to do and the women be always fightin'."

"You must have done OK," replied Mrs. Davis, "or you wouldn't have gone to the three-quarter house if you hadn't been ready."

"How does the three-quarter house differ from this rehab center?" I asked.

"Where I am now is more like home. We can come and go," replied Mercie.

Mrs. Davis explained, "They teach the people to live productive lives again. They are given a GED (General Equivalency Development) test and have a chance to get an education. Some go to work and come back to live here just as you do at home. Most of the ladies stay at the three-quarter house for around six months and then hopefully they can be on their own again."

We drove toward the place where Mercie lived; we dropped her off at the corner. Mrs. Davis reminded her to call the center for food. "I expect to see you at the Needle's Eye tomorrow!"

"That's what gets discouraging," Irma said as we drove on. "You get a woman detoxed, put into recovery, and just like Mercie, she'll go right back on the street. That's what our program is all about. Discipline, discipline, discipline! And that's so hard! It seems the devil comes with an attack and the next thing they go back on drugs. Mercie said she was lost. She wasn't lost. Standing on the street corner showed me she was wanting money to get some drugs. You saw how she flagged after the man when we first drove up."

I shook my head. I was beginning to understand.

We arrived at the detox center where Irma's daughter works as a counsellor. Even before we got into the building an elderly woman called out to Irma and came running to meet her. They jested and laughed; she told us to look around. Later I learned she is the mother-in-law of the man who runs the center.

The clinic was immaculately clean and everything seemed to run efficiently. Patients spend approximately twenty eight days here. The building is equipped to give physical examinations, has rooms for individual and group therapy, and is supplied with

hospital staff and equipment.
We left the rather isolated place and drove to another housing project; it has the reputation of being the worst one in the country. It looked the way I pictured concentration camps. There were long, monotonous, all-the-same-type houses surrounded by high woven fences. The location on a hill, made it appear massive--like endless rows of barracks. Middle-aged men, obviously out of work, stood in huddles; children, not in school, looked bored.
"I want to get out of here as soon as I can!" said my driver as she hastily turned about at a dead-end street. "My husband says a housing project is the last place he would choose to live! It's not a place to raise a family. People are too blocked in. It's inhumane!"
As we came out of the project Mrs. Davis pointed to the small church. "We brought a group of people there on the lawn to hold a street meeting last summer. We sang and played our tambourines, and passed out free hotdogs and gave away used clothing that we'd brought from the Needle's Eye."
We drove up Hillman Street and came past the junior high school just as the children were dismissed. Children came streaming out of the building, just as they do in every other town. But this was different. Mrs. Davis started talking very fast. "Do you see the junkies? You know them by their fine cars and the loud music. The rap music they're playing with the loud speakers is a signal announcing to the kids: 'Come to the curb and get your drugs.' You can hear the 'doom, doom' rhythm for as far as a mile or two away!" "Do you notice the young boys on the street corners? They're the runners. They do the running for the junkies. It's called 'clocking'. Those boys can make as much as $1,000 a week doing that. It's actually a business that is hard to bust because of the money involved.
"Did you see the transaction between the runner and the junkie? The money must be handed over before the drug is handed out. It will cost $20 for a crack half the size of your thumb nail; $40 for the full size of your nail."
"Hold it. What is a crack?" I demanded.

"A crack is a rock to be smoked in a pipe. Cocaine comes in powder form, called 'white.'"

Obviously, I was missing all kinds of things her trained eye was observing!

"Over there is the base house."

"Irma, tell me. What happens in a base house?"

"That's where kids can go and sniff the drugs in a kind of inhaler. The drugs are already mixed and ready to be inhaled. Of course, it's more expensive to do it that way."

"Look at the kids!" I gasped. "They're lined up to get into those houses!"

"'You'll soon be able to pick out the houses. It's where the kids congregate."

"So it becomes a sociable thing to do. A kind of peer pressure," I speculated.

"Exactly. It's a hard cycle to break."

"Could $\underline{I}$ go into a base house?" I asked naively.

"No, they wouldn't trust you. You're white and they'd be afraid you'd squeal on them."

As we drove from the area she pointed to a building and asked what I thought it was.

"It looks like a garage--a filling station, perhaps?"

"It's a place they sell drugs. It only has the front to fool you. This one is closed because it got busted by the police. There is another one, and there is another.

"And on this street are the hangouts for the prostitutes."

"I don't see any." Again I was exposing my ignorance!

"Well, they may not be out now, but wait until the men get off work. The women will be on the street with their pimps. Friday and Saturday nights get really busy."

"Excuse me again, Irma. But who picks up the girls?"

"Business men, lawyers, and even doctors are known to want a sensuous thrill. They're willing to pay to have a fling."

Now we were breezing down Market Street. "You're going fast," I remarked as buildings whizzed by.

"I don't loiter in these parts," said Irma. "This is where the devil worshipers hang out.

When we got to the park area she slowed down. Here's where I go walking every morning. I'm bringing you by here to show you one more place.

The park was to the left with its tall trees, trimmed grass, colorful flowers and attractive walkways.

"The place I want to show you is to the right in the brick building with bars across the windows, there by the corner. That's where they put the people who have lost their mind because of cocaine. People in there are insane and there is no hope for recovery. When I walk by here, I can hear cries coming from that building. It's pathetic to hear them! 'I want to go home!' 'Get me out of here!' Some are terrible cries of pain."

Then she grew quiet. I glanced over and saw tears streaming down her cheeks. In a very quiet voice she said, "Celia, sometimes at night I can't sleep. I think of my people. I love my people. I cry and cry until I can't cry anymore. I don't want to see them suffer so! I want to help them but feel so inadequate. I feel just the time we're getting somewhere they turn back, like Mercie. The devil knows how to get them." She paused and then, in a quivering voice, added, "The need is so great!"

I saw love mingled with concern. Tears filled my eyes and for a brief moment we wept together. Then I turned to her and said, "Irma, even the Lord focused his attention to a few at a time in most of His ministry. He stayed in a given vicinity throughout His life and look what He accomplished!"

"I know. I know. Sometimes I get discouraged. I'd like to reach so many more," she said.

"Perhaps you feel like you reach a comparatively small number of people. Look how many people you know. It seems everywhere we go they know you. Didn't you tell me you received one hundred fifty Mother's Day cards from people other than your own children this year? You're making a difference in their lives. If everyone would do as much as you it would soon change the world. Don't give up!"

"I don't plan to give up, but there is so much to do! I'll keep going till the Lord takes me home."

With this she wiped away her tears and a smile spread over her smooth, angular face.

Chapter 6
"Meet Irma Davis"

One night the phone rang. It was Irma Davis. "Celia, we're having Black History Month and Marilyn, my daughter, is doing a ballet for us. I thought you might like to come to Youngstown and see her."

I knew of Marilyn's accomplishments and was eager to see her perform. My husband, Calvin, and I had been getting to know some of the people at the Needle's Eye and going there would give us an opportunity to further our acquaintance.

We arrived in good time Saturday morning; the few people who had gathered early seemed in a festive mood. A friendly, elderly woman explained, "Sister Davis has gone in her car to pick up folks for the meeting. She's always doin' good things for people. She's one that don't just talk about it, she does 'em. You stick 'round, she'll be back soon."

One of Irma's white friends, a nurse, came to greet us. We had met previously; we chatted and in a passing remark I said, "Irma is such an interesting person. Someone ought to write a book about her. What do you think?"

"Yes, definitely!" she said enthusiastically. "She's worth

writing about! To me she is the American version of Mother Teresa. Irma loves everybody. She makes them feel they are somebody and makes them do things for themselves. She's dependent on the Lord, she's positive, very strong, looks you straight in the eye and calls the shots but people respect her because they know she's right. She has an air of authority but with compassion; and she can clown and has a charming way of saying things."

I laughed at her long description and said, "It appears there would be plenty to write about!"

The white woman laughed and said, "No problem! Actually, I've only begun telling about her. For instance, the world needs to know the beauty of Irma's heritage. Her mother adored her father, Bishop Washington, a well-educated evangelist who travelled throughout the deep South. When most blacks made an effort to get out of the deep South, their family stayed and considered it their mission. That's the way Irma is about her work here in Youngstown."

"And there is her husband, Bob, who does his own things. He's not a public person but he doesn't stop her from being one. Well, that is, unless he sees she's too tired. She listens to him when he tells her she's had enough."

I could see she wasn't finished talking about the virtues of this woman but we were interrupted. Sophia Brooks ran to meet me with an affectionate hug. We talked of the day's program. The nurse turned to *her* and said, "Sophia, if someone were to write a book about Irma, what should they say about her?"

Without hesitation, Mrs. Brooks replied, "She takes action! Irma is a powerful, dedicated, dynamic leader. She's well known for starting this program; she runs it at very low overhead. If anyone is hungry; she'll feed them. She understands chemical dependency and knows how to give people the extra step of spirituality that makes her program so effective."

People of all ages were arriving for the program. I walked about the folding chairs set by card tables covered with white paper and decorated with centerpieces of artificial flowers. On the far side of the room, tucked into the library shelf, I spotted a four-page brochure printed by the Eastminster Presbytery. The title, "Kudos for Irma Davis," caught my eye. I picked it up and read:

I wish each of you could have the opportunity of meeting this dedicated busy Christian Woman who is the director of the 'Needle's Eye,' in Youngstown. This is a Christian Counseling Center that seeks to prevent drug/alcohol abuse, to redeem drug/alcohol abusers. She deals mostly with children and teenagers.

The program provides instruction and positive experiences so that young people can build helpful peer relationships and strong Christian character that will be able to resist the attractions of drugs and alcohol.

People are treated in a caring manner that ministers to the whole person, providing necessities for physical sustenance, counseling individuals and families to restore broken relations, and praying and studying the Bible with them to meet their spiritual needs.

The next paragraph asked the question, "Where Does It Get Its Support?" I read on:

Through the prayers of concerned Christian people. Through the combined effort of Presbyterian churches in the Mahoning and Columbiana counties. Eastminster Presbytery, Ohio Conference of the United Methodist Church, support with mission funds. No tax or government or community charitable funds are used. It is a Christian enterprise, supported by Christian People. It is a member of the Southside Ministry in Youngstown. It is also a mission project of Eastminster Presbytery, Christ Church ladies. Presbyterian church ladies make soup once a month so that she may distribute it to needy families. Good clothing is always needed as well as monetary gifts.

Irma arrived and came right over to greet us. Then she hopped about greeting everyone else, showing them where to place the food they were carrying, checked on last minute details for the program, and made sure everyone had a place to sit.

Betty Robbins, one of three full-time employees of the Needle's Eye, was in charge of the long table filling up with food.

The smell of barbecued chicken wings, cornbread, chitterlings, blackbeans, homemade lemonade, sweet potato pies and all kinds of salads, mingled together into a mouth-watering aroma. The tables, covered with white paper, were beginning to sag under the weight!

Irma started the program even as folks kept coming. Everyone was shocked to attention when a train whistle was heard and Ann, Irma's daughter-in-law appeared from the backroom dressed in costume and speaking the Negro dialect of Harriet Tubman, liberator of black slaves. Next, a handsome man in his teens stepped out to impersonate Martin Luther King, Jr., the emancipator who taught the Negro people to solve problems without using violence.

A pre-med student was introduced and lauded as a former Good News clubber. One could sense the pride of the audience as she sang "Deep River" in a rich contralto voice.

When it was time for Marilyn Rose to perform, she came up the aisle with her understudies, who tried to mimic her. They could not match her form and graceful movements, but the audience didn't mind. People showed their approval by clapping their hands to the rhythm of the music. I was so wrapped in her performance that I did not notice her father, Bob Davis (who had come in late and squeezed through the crowd to sit with Calvin and me), until he leaned over and whispered, "We'll have to have the next meeting at a larger place!" We smiled in agreement.

Mrs. Davis gave thanks for the food; then in a courteous, orderly manner, everyone lined up, filled their plates and returned to eat it at their tables.

"I want you to meet Ron Foreman, a college graduate and social worker," said Bob Davis. "He volunteers his time to help at the Needle's Eye."As we smiled and shook hands I asked him who plans the programs for Black History Month.

Pointing to Mr. Davis he said, "His wife. She is the model supreme teacher here. When you're talking about not wasting a life, a catching sense of doing, changing, working, moving, you've got to be talking about Irma Davis. She makes things better. She has a dream, a vision, a philosophy that has changed

Needle's Eye

Youngstown!"

After dinner I talked with Dottie Faith, treasurer of Southside ministries, about the Needle's Eye. "The program reaches young people with an alternative life-style," she said. "The Christian message they get here is based on other values than what they get on the street. This is due to the influence of Irma Davis. She's black, she speaks their language, knows everybody, she's honest and open with them and what she tells them it makes sense. She works with families a lot. Referrals come from agencies, courts and off the street. She helps people get in touch with God. That's the secret of her success."

As Calvin and I drove out of Youngstown I was strangely quiet. "What are you thinking?" asked my husband.

"Calvin, did you notice that not one person said a bad thing about Irma? They only praise her? I can hardly believe what I heard and saw there today."

He mulled that over in his mind, then answered. "I get the impression she wouldn't be happy to hear all the praise. It seems if she knew what people were telling us, she would have said, 'Stop it! All praise goes to God! It is He that makes things happen.' "

I smiled. "Calvin, I think you are right."

Chapter 7
"Meeting and Marrying"

Irma had just poured tea into Calvin's cup and was ready to fill mine when the two burly police dogs tied to the garage behind the house raised a rumpus. They pulled at their chains and yipped as a pickup truck pulled into the drive.

"That's Bob," explained Irma. "The dogs always fuss when he comes. They can't wait to see him." The truck door slammed, Bob's keys jingled as he unlocked the house, then he came to the living room and gave each of us a hearty handshake.

"Good to see you folks," he said. "Welcome to our house." His wife hurried for another cup and saucer; he excused himself to wash his hands.

When they returned we sat and chatted. Calvin pointed outside the window. "I noticed there are two houses on the lot beside you that are being torn down. Were they old or what?"

Bob jumped to his feet and parted the curtains. "Those were both cocaine houses," he explained. "The city has a right to demolish drug houses. They came with bulldozers and got rid of them."

"It was an answer to prayer to have those houses removed!" exclaimed his wife. "We had so much trouble over there . . . Oh, I was grateful when they got rid of those houses! Now I'm praying for a couple more down the street to go."

"I was able to buy the two lots and want to make a community garden there this summer," Bob explained. "I'm in the process of cleaning up the place. I loaded up the slates that came off the roofs and today went looking for someone who'd buy them. I didn't have any luck in Akron, so I went to Cleveland to see a man who promised to buy some. He wasn't in. Guess I'll have to try again tomorrow. If not, I'll have to unload them and start at another place.

"Are you interested in looking around?" he asked Calvin. Calvin followed Bob out the front door.

I turned to Irma and said, "You have a handsome husband. How did you hook him?"

Her faced beamed and I sensed a story. We settled back and she began:

When I started getting interested in boys I was pretty large. I wore a size sixteen dress and that is big. When different boys came around I stopped eating whole pies and lost weight. I got down to a dress size twelve.

The first time I laid eyes on Bob was while I was riding to school on the city bus one morning. I knew everyone on the bus except this person who had just gotten on. I didn't pay any attention to him 'cause in our culture we never speak to strangers.

When this same young man came to our church on Sunday morning I took notice of him. We were having a song fest and I was up in the choir singing, "I've got a Home Eternal in Heaven." Our eyes met and I winked at him and he winked back at me. He came up to me after church and asked me my name. I told him, "Valerie." I knew I couldn't tell him the truth because my father wasn't going to let me talk to anyone who didn't belong to our church.

That young man came looking for me. 'Cause we lived in a small town and lived in the first house, I wasn't too hard to find. My father answered the door. There stood this young man.

My father asked his name. He said, "I'm Robert Davis. I'm looking for the girl who sings in the choir there in that church around the corner. Her name is Valerie and I'd like to talk to her."

I was cooking in the kitchen but I heard the conversation and was curious who it was. By this time my father had figured out that his girl, Nell, was having a caller. Dad caught me peeping out so he called out really loud, "Irma Nell, come here!"

When I came out I saw this boy and knew I'd been found out. I suddenly got bashful.

"Tell this boy your name," demanded my father.

In a soft voice I said, "Irma Nell."

"Speak up, please," continued my father in an orderly manner.

Robert said to Reverend Washington, "C ca can I talk to your daughter?"

My father nodded and said he could but quickly asked, "What church do you go to?"

Robert stuttered, "I b belong to the B Baptist Church."

"You understand we're Pentecostal?" asked my father. Dad wouldn't let us date anyone who wasn't of the same denomination!

"I don't know about you seeing her. She's still in school. Can't you wait until she finishes?" suggested my father.

Robert got up his courage and made a request. "C can I have her address?"

"Well, I guess so," said my father.

Robert was good looking and tall. He wore beige khaki pants and a shirt to match, country style. I liked him but didn't let on to my father. Because I considered myself a city girl I called him a "cotton picker" and a "country boy."

Robert kept coming to our church and later joined it. One girl in the choir was crazy about Robert. She told me things he had said to her but I made up my mind that he was going to be mine. I didn't care what my mother and father said, I liked him so we kept in touch. We wrote to each other. Sometimes he would have his sister write to me and she would write a love letter all about kissing and hugging. We never did all that; in fact we hadn't even kissed once.

I got a letter like that once and put it on the trunk. I wasn't trying to hide anything. My father picked it up and read it. He went on something terrible, and threatened that he wouldn't let me see Robert again.

I could always talk with my father so I said to him, "I don't care what you say. I like him and I want to marry him."

Now, in my family my oldest brother was David; next were James Lee, Sadie Elizabeth and then me, Irma Nell. My parents raised their granddaughter Pat. We took her in as a baby from the hospital when I was thirteen. Two years later we took Melba into our home when her mother passed away.

My father would always send my niece Pat along when I went on a date so she could tell him everything she heard and saw. Pat wasn't nice to Robert 'cause she knew I liked him and she was afraid she was going to lose her Nell. She'd kick and bit him in all kind of meanness.

Well, we got married when I finished school at eighteen years of age. I planned a big wedding. There were twelve bridesmaids. All the girls in the church had to be in the wedding.

I was made to learn Proverbs 31 to recite by memory before I could get married. We even made up a song about "Who can find a Virtuous Woman?"

The wedding was something else! There was foot washing, communion, singing, and preaching. I mean, we had a one-day revival!

This was a sober occasion and I was not to smile. Now when I look at my wedding picture I feel ashamed. I look like I'm going to the electric chair. I was told to look sober so I did.

After we got married we moved to Pensacola, Florida. That was a great time for us. We were close enough home that I could go home every weekend. Those girls in the church took advantage of that and came and spent the weekends with us. My husband was nice to them but he hated it. But he never complained.

I started to go to church in Pensacola. There I met a

woman named Gertrude who was a nurse. She showed me around and we became great friends. She worked in a dry cleaner and had access to a car or a station wagon. She would go up to Mobile two or three times a week to pick up laundry. Once we went to Mobile and ran out of gas just before we got back to Florida. There we sat. I was seven months pregnant with no money. Man, did I pray! As I prayed, along came an Adam's Furniture Store truck. I flagged it down and told the driver, "My name is Irma Nell. I'm Bishop Washington's daughter."

"You mean that singing girl? Oh, I'll go and get you some gas but I don't have any money," he said.

I explained where we lived and how we had run out of gas.

He remembered that my father was the man with all the faith.

We talked awhile and then he said, "I'll go and get it this time for you but next time you better have some bread."

Our first baby, Robert Junior, was born on September 30, 1951, in Our Lady of Angels Hospital. I was so happy to have such a beautiful baby! Meanwhile Robert worked on the railroad sometimes or drove a truck hauling timber.

Chapter 8
"Life in Youngstown"

Some of my neighbors, poor tenants without jobs, have no heat in their houses. Bills remain unpaid and their electricity has been cut off. They take turns going to bed to sleep; the rest have to sit up. Many don't have enough blankets to keep themselves warm!

Celia shivered to think of it! She felt the cold just stepping outside the house and here were people facing a long, harsh winter with no heat at all!

She decided to do something to help those people. After a few phone calls, the ladies of her church decided to have a blanket and food drive as part of the Thanksgiving offering. They got together and knotted a few special comforters and by the end of November they had enough blankets and food to fill a van belonging to a man in their church. You should have seen Mrs. Davis when she caught sight of the church's loaded van!

Later I asked her, "How did you decide to live in Ohio? And why did you choose Youngstown?" Her ready answer was,

"The Lord led us here." Then she sat in a contemplative mood for a while before she went on. Word came to us, when we still lived in Mobile, that a cousin of mine had been lynched on a tree. It was a painful experience to see the agony the family went through. We began wishing to get away from it . . . away from the injustices, especially now that we were thinking of raising a family of our own.

Robert is a member of the #125 Hod Carriers and Labor Union. Because he was a member, it was easy for them to transfer him to a new job. The union had a job building the Ohio Turnpike at the time and needed workers, so they transferred him from Alabama to Ohio.

We moved into my aunt's house in Youngstown, even though there was only one room available. Some Puerto Ricans lived with her. They had come to work in the steel mills. She was not married and was willing to share what she had but it was confining; it was tough living there.

Bob Jr. was still a baby in that summer of 1953. He was the apple of our eyes. He got into everything! He was perpetual motion and very smart and he kept me busy running after him.

We had two more children while we lived with my aunt. Ronald, a second son, came four years after Bob, and then we had Marilyn Rose. We were definitely crowded. It was time to move; and God blessed us with a little house with two bedrooms, a living room, and a kitchen.

In 1967 my father called and said, "Nell, come on home. I am dying."

"I can't. I don't have the money to come," I told him.

"Make reservation and leave tomorrow," he said.

I called my attorney friend and he picked up a ticket for me. "You need to go home and see your folks," he said not knowing my father had a heart attack. I prayed as I got on the plane that my father would still be alive with a good sound mind. I arrived at 4:30 in the morning, took a cab home and went into the house. He wanted me to bake him a cake, so I made a one-layer cake. He ate it, then I shaved him, and then he said, "Nell, take me to the hospital. I am so sick, I know I am going

home."
When we got to the hospital my mother and I stayed in the room with him. He called my mother to him and said to her, "You are a good woman. I love you. You are a good worker." Then he turned to me and said, "Nell, you are a strong girl. You are going to do great things for God. Go to it!" He died at 2:40 p.m.

My dad was really close to me. I was glad I was there when he died. People came from far and wide to that funeral. When I arrived home in Ohio, Bob said to me, "Now that your father has died you will be mine." You see, he had sensed that I was my dad's girl. Bob took the place of my father after that.

The Lord brought a lady named Mrs. Lyons into my life soon after we moved. She loved me and taught me many good things about parenting, canning, cooking, sewing. We made quilts and had large gardens. Mrs. Lyons was heaven-sent. She became Marilyn's godmother. And when our son Ronny got very sick with asthma we had to spend a lot of time and money on him. She was our baby sitter, helper, and literally our lifeline. She talked to me a lot about holding on to what God gave us in Alabama. "You've got to keep it!" she'd caution me.

When Ronny was twelve years old he went to the altar and claimed his own healing. It was at a revival in Pennsylvania at the Shore Front Church. Ronny went up by himself and asked the man of God to lay hands on him. He came home and said, "Mama, I am healed."

I said, "Ronny, you are just a kid. You don't know what you are saying."

But I was wrong. He was healed! In fact, later in life when he went to college out in Kansas with all those wheat fields around him, he was fine.

I remember that Ronny had a hard time learning the Lord's Prayer, so I made him write it fifty times. He put it up on the walls in his room and I heard him say, "Lord, there they are. If you want them you can have them."

Marilyn, our youngest, loved to dance. We started her on ballet lessons when she was five. When she broke her leg we gave her tap-dancing lessons, and that was therapeutic. The lessons paid off. Later in life she danced with the Western Reserve Dance Company. She went to New York and danced in <u>Laquia,</u> the <u>Nut Cracker Suite,</u> <u>Hansel and Gretel,</u> and the <u>Glow Child.</u> She continued until her marriage on August 8, 1987.

My sons played football, ran track, played hockey and basketball. It was great discipline. If it had not been for sports my sons would not have had an education. They received both grants and scholarships that helped pay for their education because they did so well in sports.

You see, I decided to let God guide me on how to bringing up my kids. Of course I disciplined them. Whenever the boys in our house had to have a licking, Marilyn, our only girl, would run up and down the stairs praying. She sure would do a lot of praying whenever the boys were being punished.

I started looking around to see what God wanted me to do with me besides going to church and working so I started a prayer group. We called it the Deliverance Prayer Band. In it were most of the mothers whose kids played football or Little League baseball or were cheerleaders. Soon most of the parents joined us; we prayed every Wednesday.

The children's mothers and I became great friends. We did all kind of things. To every game I took candied apples or sometimes just plain ones and passed them out to all the teams. They called me the apple lady. It was my way of letting people know who I was by having contact with them.

At one time seven boys lived in our house besides my own family. They treated my daughter as their own sister. I saw that what they needed was an organized club for boys only. In 1971 we organized a club and called it the "Execs" short for "Executives." They'd come to our house every Sunday because they'd get good cooking. I would cook a canning-pot full of spaghetti, and serve great big bowls of salad and three or four pies or cakes. I enjoyed doing it and, of course the boys liked it! After a while they met in other homes too. But when the Execs came to our house I always made them pray. There were twenty two boys in that group. Some of them dropped out, but from that group came four ministers, and most of the rest of the boys are saved. I believe that those who aren't will some day turn to the Lord because they know the way.

Each August, when my mother would come up, she'd make cheerleaders' outfits. One time they wanted blue and white outfits. I went into the second-hand store and got some old drapes. We made a pattern from newspaper and made blue and white skirts that had flares. We bought white socks that looked great with the skirts.

I also started visiting the Mahoning County Nursing Home. I'd take my kids and a few of their friends out there to sing. Many of the women got saved, so we would have a service on Good Friday and on Easter. One of the ladies thought it would be a good idea to give the residents communion, so we started doing that once a year. We would take dyed eggs to them at Easter, candy at Christmas time, and have a special Memorial Day service in May.

Once we took the old people from one of the rest homes into the park. Some ran away from us, so we changed parks and went to Lincoln Park, where there is a big hill. That way we could watch them better, and it had better restroom facilities.

Whenever we went we'd take the residents out of their rooms and have prayer services, singing, and have lots and lots of food, including homemade ice cream. The next year we added five more nursing homes to our schedule. This activity is still continuing today.

In May 1987 we celebrated our twenty-sixth year visiting rest homes. We held special services but this time at the Needle's Eye. When my children got to high school they talked me out of having meetings for the older folks all the time for it was taking too much time. The children attended the South High School. There was no school spirit at South Side, so I decided they needed a Booster Club. The first meeting was in our home one Sunday night; then we moved it to the Friendship Baptist Church and worked out of there raising money by selling food at each football game. We had a minister go into the field house and pray before each game. After the game we fed the boys who played on the school team.

The Booster Club would clean up the stadium after the football game, run the concession stand, and sell hot dogs and pop. With the money we earned we were able to get uniforms, equipment for the football field, and suits for kids who didn't have any for graduation. It helped to have one of the white men, a lawyer, stand by us whole-heartedly while we worked. He and I both looked at issues that concerned our children. Both his and my children were in South High, said to be the worst school in the whole city. He kept his kids there and we kept ours there. When his son, a football player, began drinking he wouldn't let him play.

I was impressed by his strong discipline. His wife and I got along well too. We'd get together and cook large meals for the many young people who kept coming to the Davises'. We had a pool table in our basement, and kids who couldn't go home would come to our house. All kinds of kids hung out down in our basement. I heard and saw everything! I heard about drugs, who was having sex, or who was having a baby. Some of the kids were runaways. When I found out I would send them home. I became a person to whom both teachers and children could talk. One of those boys, two years younger than my son, got onto heroin and became an addict. That boy joined the Army but got kicked out; his parents were devastated!

I visited the parents of the kids who came to our home and learned of the drug problem in the schools. Students were shooting drugs into their arms without knowing how to do injections. They didn't know the difference between different drugs, or how the drugs would interact.

Then a child on my street was injected with drugs incorrectly and he died a terrible death. That infuriated me! Kids were injecting themselves with drugs more and more and I didn't have the know-how, the tools to work with, to help them.

One day I put on a big breakfast for our son Ron after his prom. There were drunk kids all over the place. I didn't kick them out; I just loved them and kept them there until they got sober. If students arrived at our house drunk, I prevented them from driving home. That meant I had to feed them, and they'd sleep on the floor in the basement. By early afternoon I'd make them go home. It was to this prom that Cathy, Ronny's girl (the one he later married), wasn't allowed to go unless her father was hired to be the policeman at the door. My friend Betty Robbins and I went to that prom all dressed up in a formal African dress that looked every bit as good as the brand named dashiki! We didn't go to bother the kids, only to watch what went on. We stayed there all night and that's why all the kids came to our house the next morning. This after-prom party at our house started a real friendship between us and the young people. After ten years they still talked about that after-prom party and how a lot of them had been drunk and how we'd love them in spite of it.

Everyone who came to our house got exposed to the gospel. We'd sing and beat tambourines and pray together.

I decided that once our sons and daughter were all in college I would become a missionary. All my life I had wanted to be a missionary; I wanted to go to Africa. God had other plans for me. He let me know that my mission field was right here in the inner city of Youngstown, Ohio. I'm glad I heeded God's call because it seems to me there is plenty of work to do here.

Many women who may have three or four children, come up to me and say, "Irma, the Lord has called me to the mission field."

I tell those women, "You have four foreigners living with you right now. Work with them! Nothing should be more important to you than to raise them first."

Irma's Roots.

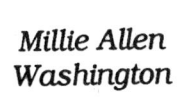

Millie Allen
Washington

Bishop David
Washington

BEHOLD

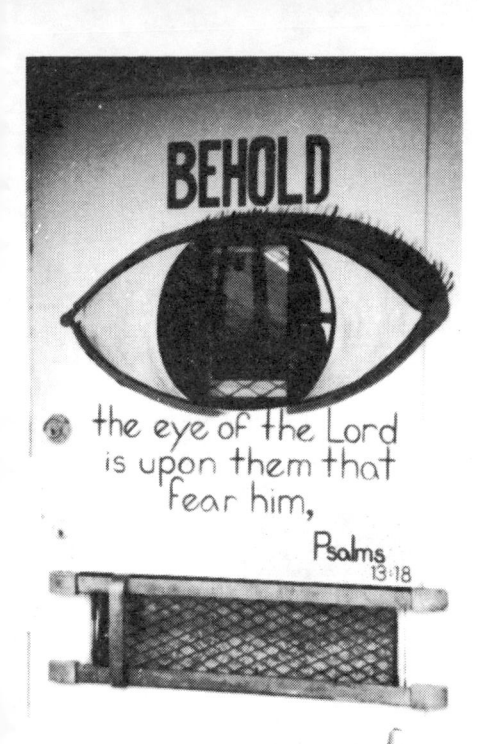

the eye of the Lord is upon them that fear him,

Psalms 13:18

THE NEEDLE'S EYE
CHRISTIAN COUNSELING CENTER
Smile - GOD Loves You!

I promise to lead a drug-free life. I want to stay healthy and happy. I will say NO to harmful drugs. I will help my friends say NO to drugs. I promise to stand up for what I know is right.

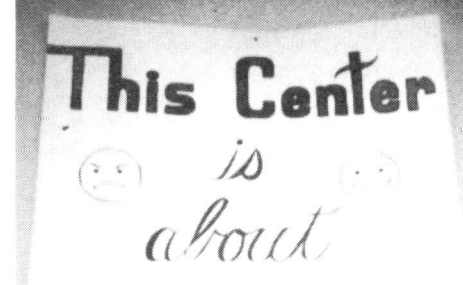

This Center is about Discipline!!!

Irma Nell and Robert Davis

Irmas says, "The Kids Are Worth The Hassle"

Impersonating Harriet Tubman

Going to the DuSable Museum of African-American History

Chapter 9
"The Needle's Eye"

I'd wanted to be a missionary in Africa but I saw the need in Youngstown; I felt that God wanted me to stay right where I was and do something about the drug problem that was getting out of hand. Even one of my own relatives, a cousin whom my children admired so much, was on drugs. He died a terrible death because of heroin.

It was time for someone to do something about it! I started going to seminars that were offered. I read everything I could find on the topic. I talked to people who had a problem. I sent notice to the <u>Youngstown Vindicator</u>, our city paper, and said I would have a meeting in my home for people who needed counselling.

When people started coming to the counselling sessions, I saw that I, myself, needed help. Community folks were meeting at the John Knox Presbyterian Church on Market Street to enroll their children in an enrichment academy called "Happiness House," so I went with my children and began talking to people about the drug and alcohol problem. Someone suggested we call a special meeting.

We did have a meeting to discuss what to do and lots of people showed up! I stood up and suggested that we rent a store front right in the worst section of town where the pimps and prostitutes were working the street, where junkies were peddling their drugs. "That's where we need to start the counselling center!" I said.

Some folks said, "Ah, that will never work!"

Others said, "I'm not sure about that."

One man, Reverend Richard Braun, minister at the John Knox Church, was more optimistic. "I think it's worth a try," he said. "I'll round up a few chairs and desks for the project." Rev. Braun was like that. He was willing to try new things and saw virtue in having black and white people working together on a project.

I was nominated to head the project. With the promise of support, I got busy, rented a store front at 2219 Hillman Street, and went into that wilderness of sin saying, "If the Lord is with me, I can do all things through Christ!" So it was from the very beginning I was director of the work.

Our group fixed up the place and soon we were open for business.

I was shaken when I saw who showed up! It was the children--dirty, full of lice, unkempt. One seven-year-old was drunk. Some children said they hadn't been to bed the night before.

I saw that I needed help. I hurried to the phone and called Sara Weaver, a long-time friend who had been working with inner-city kids in Youngstown who now lived seventeen miles away. I begged her, "Please come and help. I need you! These children need the gospel and bad! Can you come and teach?"

She came. Thirteen children sat and listened while Sara placed colorful pictures of David and Goliath on the flannel board. We talked to the children and learned that many were cold and hungry, so we fed them. We went to the Presbyterian Church and asked for blankets.

The children streamed into the meetings every Saturday

morning. We taught them discipline and self-worth, but mainly we taught them about the Lord. Our lessons were geared to children aged five years and up; we called ourselves the Good News Club.

That summer we had our first Bible school. It wasn't like any vacation Bible school you ever heard of! We had fifty children and we gave them breakfast. I believe in cleanliness, so before they ate we had a wash basin, towel and clean-up rags, and plenty of soda and soap to get them clean. We made sure all the children were clean and smelled good. Four girls, friends of my children, fixed the little girls' hair. They washed it, corn-rowed it, and put beads in it to make it look pretty! We gave them new clothes and shoes that our children had gathered. Finally we gave them the gospel.

We took our club to the football hall of fame and to the zoo. We took them to Sara's Mennonite farm for a first look at cows and would go every year to the Westminster Church for a Halloween party. Westminster would have lots of hot dogs, pizza, soup and beans. The word got around and more kids came. As many as forty kids would show up, sometimes more. They came from broken homes, addicted homes, abusive homes. All needed discipline. We believed that if we could get a child into our program by the time he was five, and if we could get the gospel into him and put discipline in him, he would make it.

We needed a name for our place on Hillman Street. Mr. John Sharick, a man on our committee, came up with the name "Needle's Eye." He based it on Luke 18:25, in which a rich young man came to Jesus seeking salvation. Jesus knew that the young man trusted in his riches and as long as he did that he'd never make it. Jesus said to the young man, "It is easier for a camel to go through the eye of a needle than for a rich man to enter the kingdom of heaven."

We all liked his suggestion. The more we thought about it the more it seemed to fit. We were dealing with burdened-down people who would never make it into the kingdom of God unless they unburdened themselves at the feet of Jesus and changed their life style.

The Needle's Eye would be a redemptive center for anyone wanting to be freed from alcoholism, cocaine, or other drugs, from prostitution, abuse or anything that was burdening them. There we would provide instruction and positive experiences so that those who came through the Needle's Eye could develop into Christians who would be able to resist the attractions of the world and the temptations around them.

Working with children was fine; but what about all the dope addicts, the prostitutes, the pushers? They were still out there on the street, unreached.

A group of us brought together some hot dogs and drinks and homemade soup. We equipped ourselves with tambourines, our Bibles, and the food we had prepared. We prayed for courage and took to the street! First we needed to get people's attention, so we sang and beat our tambourines. When a small crowd gathered we preached and we passed out free food.

That got their attention! One man came wanting money for drugs. When we refused he became demanding. I looked him in the eye and sent him across the street, where he started a fight. We called the cops.

We didn't do anything without a lot of prayers and fasting first. The work had to be the Lord's and not ours. We soon had a rapport with policemen who trusted us and responded when we called them. We began working with children's services and the welfare departments, and they began referring people to us.

One day we had a street meeting in Hilliam Street Park. Sara Weaver did all the teaching. When a young man stole her purse she said calmly, "Don't worry about it. I'll give it over to the Lord."

I was ashamed and angry because it had happened in my community to a dear woman who had come seventeen miles to help us.

Later the young man was sent to prison for another misdemeanor. Five years later he told me what he had done with the purse. "I put it in the street manhole," he said. He wanted to go with me to her house to apologize. He said to her, "Ms. Sarah, you are a saint. You didn't have me put in jail. I went anyway.

I want you to forgive me."
 He is still out in the world of sin but God told me that the young man will come to him.
 One time a cocaine user came into the Needle's Eye. He had just finished "free-basing" in one of the houses where addicts went to breathe the cocaine through masks. Through God-given insight I said to him, "Come in here and be safe. You see, I know what your have done. God let me that know if you don't get help right away you will die."
 I had learned that he had gotten some bad drugs that another man had used, and he had overdosed. The hospital had brought him back to consciousness but he needed further help. God sent him to the Needle's Eye for a cup of coffee and it saved his life. Because he got into treatment, he's alive today and testifying about God.

Chapter 10
"What's Going On?"

    The people in my congregation were in for a surprise! The Sunday evening program was completely in charge of the founder of the Needle's Eye. Irma came with two dozen of her people who, drove two and a half hours to share their story with us.
    It was my thinking, as program chairman, that it would be good for our sheltered, conservative, Christian community to have some exposure to the happenings of the inner city. Our mode of worship is singing four-part-harmony hymns, heavy Bach chorals on the organ, and gospel preaching, but our people are open to new modes of worship and try to understand cultural differences.
    The visiting group was well prepared to lead the worship service. The youth started the program with rap songs and scripture. Then Sophia Brooks sang, in an exuberant voice that filled the huge sanctuary with "Deep River." She accompanied herself on the piano.
    At this point Irma introduced Jackie White to the congregation. "When Jackie first came to the Needle's Eye she was carrying a gallon of whiskey with her. Her feet were swollen, she was spitting up blood,and was a very, very sick woman. But

the Lord delivered her. I'll let her tell you her story."

"Everything Mrs. Davis said about me is true," the attractive woman in her early thirties began. "When I first went to the Needle's Eye for help I was hallucinating. When Mrs. Davis brought me a plate of spaghetti and meat balls everything moved around on the plate! The spaghetti looked like live worms; the meatballs had a horrible green color. It was awfully frightening! I knew I needed help.

"She put me in a detox program in the hospital for three weeks. Then they placed me in rehab. It was a pretty place. I could work, get education, have group therapy and individual counseling. I needed all of those. Since that time I have lived ten years in sobriety. I went back to my former job. My husband died and I do not have the children; I live alone but I am on a spiritual walk with the Lord. When I get low I call Mrs. Davis or go see her. It keeps me going."

Irma thanked our congregation for the blankets, apples and eggs. She gave a brief summary of what the Needle's Eye is and how it was named. Then she glared at the audience, got their attention and let them have it with both barrels!

"You want to know what life is like in the city? I'll tell you! Last week a junkie, high on drugs, came into The Needle's Eye. He pointed a gun at my head and said, 'I'm gonna' shoot off your head, woman!'

"I put a finger in the junkie's face and said, 'What kind of a mother have you got to raise a son that pulls a gun on an old woman? I have a son just your age and any woman who doesn't teach her boy better respect ought to be ashamed. Now put that gun down and come back here. We're going to pray the devil out of you.

"The junkie lowered his gun and followed. The counsellors and I prayed and prayed and prayed for that man, and he got the victory. Praise God!

Irma placed her hands on her hips and asked, "Was I scared? 'Course I was scared. But I think of God's power in me. Why, it's much greater than the devil's power in that man. It gave me strength to stand tall.

"Did I report him? You better believe I did! The police officers know our work and stand behind us.

"The same week that happened, I learned of the attempted murder of a white child. The attempted murderers shot at a little boy lying in his crib. He was hit but wasn't killed because the grandparents who heard the shot came into the bedroom and scared the devil worshipers away before they got the baby. The news media reported that those who fired the gun wanted a blonde child with blue eyes for an offering on the devil's altar.

"When I heard about this I went to investigate where these satan worshipers meet. I found the place on Market Street. It was an ordinary looking place where many people had gathered. I went there but I didn't say a word. There were too many of them and they would have overpowered me. I only looked.

"Both of those stories are drug-related," she said. "I could tell you many more. Maybe you're saying right now,'We don't have drug problems where we live.' You may be surprised. Nobody deliberately starts out to be an alcoholic or drug abuser.

"I'm going to list the definite behavior pattern of people who become dependent on drugs.

"One. At the beginning of a habit they begin to rationalize: 'I don't want to do this but once won't matter. I can control myself.'

"Two. Their personality begins to change. They stay in their rooms, find different friends, get more secretive.

"Three. They won't accept what others say and aren't as productive in their work.

"Four. Denial. 'I don't have a problem!' they say or make excuses.

"Five. Negative thinking becomes a norm; they are still convinced they can stop if they want to.

"Six. Drugs becomes their love affair. Drugs become more important than work or commitments.

"Seven. They become less friendly with people; family and friends are avoided.

"Eight. Drugs are taking control. Addicted, they are already thinking about the next fix before the original one is gone.

"Nine.
They admit they use drugs, and make plans for more drugs.
"Ten.
Tolerance gives way to violence.
"Eleven. They don't like themselves. They hate the drug but can't stop.
"Twelve. They crave drugs more than anything! Nothing else matters.
"Thirteen. Life falls apart. There is impaired thinking at all times. Hallucinations become frightening to them.
"Fourteen. Spirituality goes.
"Fifteen. Relationships are gone; there is moral degradation.
"Sixteen. There is bizarre behavior, and financial ruin.
"At this point there are three options: They go insane, die or recover.
"If they choose help, there is hope. The first step to recovery is to admit there is a problem and ask for help. And that's where our program comes in. We are there to help people on their road to recovery. Sorry to say, it takes about as long to recover completely as it took them to become addicted.
"I remember the first case; he came to my house on Easter Sunday. My friend, who is a writer and minister, brought a boy who was on drugs. That boy couldn't eat; he could only drink pop. My daughter offered him some steak. He tried to eat it and became wild. He ran around the house, up and down. He gagged with dry heaves, ran to the bathroom, raced up and down the stairs. Finally he lay on the couch and wouldn't move. We gave him some ginger ale which immediately came back up. We began to pray for him. He knew it was not safe for him to go outside because his customers were looking for him. He had furnished the drugs for them and if he wouldn't give them more they would kill him. We had to get him out of town! The street gang knew his car and it wasn't safe for him to drive it on the street. We called the man who had brought him and asked him to help us. This man was able to lead him out. It was a miracle how that boy was delivered from addiction that day! Today he is

married and has a good job in Cleveland.

"One day the street was full of children coming home from school. You have to remember that around the center are mostly black and Spanish people. One little white West Virginian boy was being chased by fifty of the neighborhood children out to kill him. He ran into the Needle's Eye and we hid him in the women's bathroom.

"When the kids came in to find him they wanted to know where we hid him. I looked blank. 'Where is who?' I asked.

"By this time the boys went to the basement and the girls went to the women's bathroom to look for him. I held my breath! They looked everywhere but couldn't find him. Then I got scared wondering what had happened to the kid.

"The kids left and out walked Billy. I said, 'Where were you?'"

'I was in the women's bathroom behind the door. I was standing behind the door when they came in but I guess they didn't see me. I think God covered me up so they couldn't see me.'

"We kept Billy there about two hours and took him home to his parents. The next day I went to the school and reported the incident. Each day after that they kept Billy after school for his safety."

I smiled as I looked at our congregation. They seemed to be enjoying Irma's stories and she seemed to be full of them!

"On a twelve-below-zero day just two of us were in the Needle's Eye. I heard a car pull up to the front of the building and stop. No one got out so I waited. You see, we are always alert and listening. I poured some coffee in a cup just so I could go outside and pour it out, so I could see who was in that car.

"A man was sitting in the car looking at our door. I waved to him to come in. He let his window down.

"I said, 'Can I help you?'"

'Yes, I'm waiting on those nuns to come out of there,' he said as he pointed toward our building.

"I said, 'There's no one in there but George and me.'

"He looked funny and said, 'When I pulled up they went

in there. They had on black with big hats, came from that way, and came in there,' again pointing to our building.

"I finally convinced him to come in and see for himself. By now I was cold and glad to get in.

"He looked around and said, 'You let them out the back door.'

"I said, 'If I had, you would have heard me let them out. You can't open this door without hammering it open.'

"He began hammering at the door so loud it was heard in the front of the building. You could hear him talking about how he came to get the so-and-so women who had put his woman away in treatment.

"You see, when we heard all the goings on, we felt secure because this building had been blessed by a man of God at its opening. So I believed that if this man had come to do us harm that God would take care of us. Undoubtedly He sending angels in the forms of nuns to protect us. This man who came to do us harm got scared to death and left, saying, 'This is too deep for me. I'm getting out!'

"Some of our dealings with people are successes; others are failures. We do the best we can and leave the results to God.

"One girl came in for a cup of coffee to get away from her pimp on the corner. She had given him the excuse that she needed to use the bathroom. I put her in my car, and we hid her for four days. I called Kansas New Life for girls and sent her out there. Now she is saved, has two children, and she and her husband, who is a deacon, work for Jesus.

"The Holy Spirit taught me a new phase of my ministry one day when a new girl came in for treatment. I was sitting and loving these folks who came in and I did not notice this man sitting in our building watching everything we were doing in our program. When he saw a beautiful girl, who was a heroin addict, he paid attention to everything we were saying and doing.

"When I sent her across town to get a chest X-ray, she and this man made some kind of motion or something. They got together and in four days he had married her and had her on the street working. She is not well yet, and is in the women's prison.

The lesson I learned from that was to always look out. Satan is watching, like the Bible says, to snatch an opportunity to turn it into something evil. I must not be so busy praying to forget to look around.

"Sometimes I think the devil sends his folk to hurt us. One day a very large woman with a Jamaican accent started cursing us. We prayed for her. She wanted food, so we gave her food; she looked at me and started to scream and laugh and jerked at the cross I had hung around my neck.

"She said she wanted to go to Cleveland; I was happy to comply with her wishes! I told my helpers to take her to the bus depot. She laughed and laughed and screamed. The women prayed authority over her and over the evil spirit within her. We took her to the bus station but she refused to get on the bus. She said she was a witch but we were not afraid. The power of God moved for us and she left.

Mrs. Davis shifted from story telling to the organizational system of power. "I had learned growing up that in order to stay alive you had to learn the system. In the system you grab for things, and you try desperately to care for yourself because no one else is there to help you, no not even your parents. You have to fight to survive!

"Everything is to your disadvantage. Your adversary, whether it be the devil, the social service agency, or even your neighbor, always implies that you're no good. They say, 'You'll never get off welfare, you haven't got insurance, you can only go to this certain doctor or that certain dentist. You'll never make it. You'll be just like your mother.'

"How can those people make it if nobody trusts them and they're always put down? They haven't got a choice! When I work with them I try to put trust in them. I tell them they <u>are somebody</u>! I ask them what they want to do and if they say 'a nurse' or something noble I tell them to go for it, that they can make it.

"Folks who are always put down learn to get greedy. They resist being classified. They hate for anyone to make blanket statements such as 'All black people will stay on drugs, that's the way they are,' or tell them what to do as though they couldn't decide for themselves.

"Because I grew up with this, I can understand the addicted person who tries to get everything possible from you. They're always surprised I can see through what they're trying to do and understand their feelings."

The program was over. Our church's social committee had refreshments ready in Fellowship Hall. I watched as our congregation mingled with the visitors.

Chapter 11
"Fireside Chat"

There was no communication for quite a few months. Both Irma and I were busy in our own whirl of activities. One night the phone rang. It was Irma. "Celia, I need a break. Would it be possible for me to come to your house a day or two just to get away?" she asked.

"You're welcome. When do you want to come?"

"Friday night and stay till Saturday afternoon."

"Good. I'll look for you. Supper is served at five thirty."

By now Irma seemed like one of the family. Having her come only meant throwing one more potato into the pot and setting another plate on the table.

She came; after supper we had time to relax, shake off our shoes, get comfortable, and talk randomly.

"You're busy," I said starting the conversation. "Tell me about your schedule. What happens each week at the center?"

"We're open every day Monday through Saturday from ten a.m. to five thirty p.m., during which time people come for counseling. Our regular scheduled activities include the Good News Club each Saturday for the children.

"Yes, I've been there. It's a good program."

"Monday night from five to seven the youth ages eleven to eighteen meet for CIA."

"CIA?"

"That stands for Changing Into Adulthood. We saw there was too big a difference in the age groups. We needed to talk to the teen-agers about sexuality and things that concerned them. The younger ones weren't ready for that yet."

"Makes sense."

"Every Tuesday and Thursday from three thirty to five at the John Knox Church under the southside ministry, of which we are a part, there are special tutorial classes for reading and math.

"The same evening from seven to eight at the Needle's Eye there is an Alcohol Anonymous group that we call 'Sobriety First.' That program started when one of my former clients came back and said she'd like to start an AA meeting. I told her to go ahead but questioned how she planned to run it. She told me she wanted women to commit to a program where they put their sobriety first. She wanted them to be sober first. It was a good idea so that's how we do it.

"Thursday evening we have a prayer concert."

"Did you say prayer <u>concerns</u>?" I inquired for clarification.

"No, we call it a <u>concert</u>. You know how a symphony orchestra is made up of various types of instruments? In a prayer concert one may sing a praise, another calls for help, others pray for requests. It's like a musical composition."

"That's unique. Never heard it called that."

"Every Friday we meet with the parenting group at ten fifteen a.m. where we teach basic skills in home making and child rearing."

"I imagine that opens the door to a lot of activity. No wonder you're tired!" I said.

"I don't do all that myself. We constantly recruit people to help us. God lets me know who is qualified and I ask them to come."

"You mentioned the children and the women. How about the men? Do you have meetings for them?" I asked.

"That's our most recent addition. Right now we're running a Twelve Step support group meeting for the men. Ten or more men meet every Tuesday evening at seven p.m. with their leader, Mr. George Smith. Sometimes he sings for them. He's an excellent soloist.Sometimes we cook a meal, set up the tables with silver and everything, then leave it there and they really enjoy that! If the men need clothing we provide that for them.

"Mr. Smith uses the holistic view, meaning he stresses the spiritual as well as the physical, in the discussions. He uses the Bible right along with the Twelve Steps. Bibles are furnished for both the men's and the women's group by a local business man and his wife.

"Those men always have open discussion. In this group some of the men are asked to lead the meeting. Some of the men have asked to be baptized; they were taken to a church for this.

"After the twelve weeks are up they will need to decide whether to continue or drop this group; or they may start another group according to the need. Maybe by then it will be a NA or CA meeting."

"Meaning . . ."

"Oh. She stopped short, forgetting my unfamiliarity with her abbreviations. 'NA' stands for narcotic anonymous; 'CA' for cocaine anonymous. Society often doesn't realize that people on drugs are taking mind-altering substances. What our program does is to restore addicts to their right mind."

"Do you guarantee success?" I asked out of curiosity.

"Sometimes yes, sometimes no."

"I've seen many people come off drugs and alcohol and stay sober awhile and then start drinking again. That is because they don't have spirituality. This summer I worked with a young man who wore an overcoat and boots in the middle of summer. His mind was gone. I agreed with everything he said, and didn't argue with him. If he'd say, 'Where are your coat and overshoes?' I'd say I didn't have them with me.

"Then he'd say, 'I can get you some used gloves for seventy five cents,' I'd ask him where.

"Now what if this man came into a Christian setting?" she

asked.

"We'd probably say he's crazy, and stay clear of him," I said.

"Will you reach him? No. You have to go where he is. You can't tell him he's crazy, that it's hot outside, not cold. It's not easy working with such people. You've got to do a lot of praying. You have to ask the Holy Spirit to tell you how to present yourself to them.

"The AA, NA, and CA are good programs because they show fellowship and love. Many times we don't want to talk to these people. We'd rather go the other way and not shake their hands. Certainly not hug them! I could not become effective with these people until I learned to touch and hug them. People need it desperately! Unfortunately, hugging today represents lust. At the Anonymous meetings people hug each other. There is a demonstration of togetherness and caring. The new friends rally around them and give them personal attention."

"I see I have lots to learn," I interjected.

"Well, isn't it true? In too many churches you have to be dressed *just so* to be all right. Not so in the Anonymous groups. We accept them just as they are and try first of all to meet their needs. I'm sorry to say that too often if a Christian and a non-Christian are in a room together the Christian takes over and has all the answers. I've learned that sometimes we need to be quiet. We need to listen--it takes a lot of listening!

"People on drugs think they are somebody. The drug has given them that feeling. That's why they use drugs. Addicts are sensitive. If you don't remember them they are hurt. It's very important to notice them. Eye contact, looking at them first, then working with them is the right approach. Touch them! Hug them!

"They may be stinking--no matter. You sit down and give them food, and eat with them. They may really stink but I still sit and eat with them."

"Wow! You're really asking a lot," I said. "You mean to say I need to let such people ride in my new car?"

"Hey, not only ride in it, but clean up the vomit when they get sick! You need to be willing to give them your coat."

"Oh! No wonder you're a success if you're willing to do all that!" I shook my head in amazement.

"I stand back and marvel at how the Lord leads us from one thing to another if we are faithful to Him. As I said before, I was going everywhere learning how to help people. No one but alcoholics are to attend the AA meetings. When I'd attended those meetings I couldn't honestly say, 'I'm a recovering alcoholic,' so I'd say, 'I'm Irma Davis and I'm a recovering sinner.' It got me in the door of Alcohol Anonymous.

"I appears to me that if you make yourself available to the Lord things really begin to happen."

"You're right," said Irma. "In 1977 a heroin addict came into our home, he owed a lot of money to the Mafia. I went and talked to one of the big men and told him this man had given his life to God and that man give him a chance to pay off the debt. That young man gave his life to God and is living a safe and sober life. With God's help it can be done.

"The youngest alcoholic I worked with was a seven-year-old boy. He came into our program for about five years. The mother and grandmother were both alcoholic. But he got himself together and finished high school.

"That boy's sister was in the Good News Club and the teacher asked her what she wanted to be."

'I want to be a prostitute,'he said.

'Why do you want to be that?'asked the teacher.

'Because they make plenty of money.'

"The sad part of the story is that when she was thirteen she had a baby and is fifteen now and is fixing to have another one. We worked with this family for a year already and only one of the six children have responded positively.

"We are always on the lookout for ways we could reach people. One time Sara and I felt like the Lord wanted us to do some ministering at the Canfield Fair, a very large fair. I went to the management; they said we could come but we would need a tent. We didn't have money to rent a tent. I was working for an undertaker at the time and I knew about the tents used at funerals, so I asked if we could use one.

"There was a problem with the tent. Over the top was the name of the cemetery. We solved that by putting it on the back and then we put posters over the sign. Matter of fact, we had posters over the whole tent!

"When the time came we went equipped with our Bibles, tracts, and materials to teach the gospel on flannel board. We were there every day and every night, witnessing.

"This was at a time when many Hippies was turning to Jesus. They called themselves Jesus People. Most of them were white. They joined us and we'd sing and play tambourines. We had church in the tent.

"I met a woman named Patricia. She was a tough woman, a fair bum--that means she slept with all the men who worked the fair that summer. We led her to the Lord!

"Fifteen years later a woman came up to me and said, 'Are you Irma?'

"I said, 'Yes, why?'

" 'I hardly knew you,' she said to me. 'You lost so much weight.'

'Yes, I know. I've had some health problems.

"All the time I'm wondering who this woman is. We kept talking she said, 'You led me to the Lord at this fairground fifteen years ago.'

'I did?' I said.

"She told me all about what was going on. 'You know what? That day I accepted the Lord. I slept in your old ragged tent. Now I am married, have four children and am a lady minister. I come here every year looking for you.' We had a great reunion in the Lord!

"Another time, my son Ronny had a friend named Davey.

"I said to Davey, 'Come and go with me to Jesus.'

'Oh, no. I've got to work.'

"The meetings to which I invited him were in Pennsylvania.

Needle's Eye Page 81

I came home on Saturday to get supplies, and ran into him again. "I need you to help me carry some wood and supplies over to the Jesus meetings in Mercer, Pa. Can you help me?" I asked.
"Well, I'll take you but I've go to come back.'
"Oh,' I said.
"We went and when he saw all those people there. He decided to stay awhile. I told me we'd take our blankets and sit in front of the stage.
"Andre Crouch started playing 'I Don't Know Why Jesus Loves Me.' I looked at Davey and saw he was starting to melt. Andre had an altar call by singing 'It Won't Be Long, We Will Be Going Home.'
"We stayed to hear Brian Rudd preach. Davey just couldn't get away as he had planned and we stayed until Saturday night. Suddenly he was missing his billfold with his pay in it.
"We looked and looked, went to the lost and found, tore up his car looking. No billfold. We came home without it.
"He stayed with us overnight so he could go back again with us in the morning. I prayed most of the night. I was upset to think we were at a camp meeting with saved folk and someone had stolen or picked his pocket.
"The next morning I was wiped out. It was time to go to Pennsylvania and as I was getting outside to unlock the car, and there on his seat was his billfold!
"Talk about a time of rejoicing! To this day I wonder where it came from. God did it. He saw it as a miracle and God blessed him. So now his faith in God is still working. Today, Davey is a minister, preaching the Word of God."
"Irma, there is something I've been wanting to ask you a long time," I said as I filled our teacups. "What is the secret ingredient that makes your program different from other programs? Why are you successful in getting people off drugs and keeping them there? I want you to tell me this secret in one word."
"Spirituality!" she said without thinking twice.
"Spirituality," I repeated after her. "Care to define that for me?"

"To me spirituality means there is a growth process. It moves in the direction of our faith. There is hope for a way out of the mess you're in, and it can be fixed through a spiritual program. We're not completely lost! By looking to God we can find the way.

"The Needle's Eye has blessed so many as we work for the Lord in building the kingdom of God on earth. We have a great message going out to the AA community and drug community about redemptive and supportive counselling that we provide for them."

EMPTY HANDS

One by one, He took from me,
All the things I valued most.
Until I stood there empty-handed,
Every glittering Toy (drugs) was lost.
And I walked earth's highways
In all my rags and poverty
Till I heard His voice inviting,
"Lift your empty hands towards Me."

So I turned my hands toward Heaven
And He filled them with a store of His
own transcendent riches, Till they could
contain no more. And at last I comprehended
with my stupid mind and soul,
That God can not pour His riches into
Hand already full.

by a man who
called himself "Dog"

Chapter 12
"Twelve Steps"

Finding the Needle's Eye with a change in address from Hillman Street to a location closer to downtown at 74 Kenmore caused me some problems. A man on the street was able to direct me to the exact spot.

The new one-story place had the same large black letters reading THE NEEDLE'S EYE along with a picture of a smiley face and a thread running through a needle at the top--a replica of that on the other store-front building on Hillman. Instead of a large window boarded up with wood, the front was made of cement blocks painted white. The entrance door had a small window at eye level that resembled a human eye. Around the opening were words "BEHOLD the eye of the Lord is upon them that fear him. Psalms 13:18."

I tugged at the door, which felt locked. When I got it open and stepped inside, my attention immediately focused on a massive bright mural of Martin Luther King, Jr., surrounded by children from many parts of the world; it depicted his dream of equality on earth.

There was a class in session to the left, behind the

moveable room divider. I skirted it to the right and saw Irma's office toward the back. It was a cubicle with two steps ascending between walls that reached partway to the ceiling. I was standing in the right half of the main room. The restrooms, a small storeroom and the kitchen were in the back. There was a place to hang coats along with a desk and office chair tucked into the corner of the back room to form another counselling center. The place appeared sparkling clean.

Everywhere I looked I saw hand-made posters listing advice in the form of ten commandments, or warnings. There were huge burlap banners with photographs of activities sponsored by the Needle's Eye. The square metal chairs had plastic-covered seats. There were plants, a piano, a small electronic organ, a television, and shelves for books and equipment around the edges of the main room which was about forty feet by forty-five.

The ladies were seated by tables with folding chair around supporting metal posts. Florescent lights lit the room. There was an atmosphere of busyness and friendliness about the place.

As I moved toward Irma's office I was greeted by the two hostesses, who sat at a table opposite the base of the steps. They were on hand to answer the telephone, prepare craft items, organize papers or, it appeared, on call for Irma. They informed me that Mrs. Davis was counselling a young mother, and that Emaline Smith was in a meeting with the "Warriors," a women's Twelve Step support group.

"Warriors?" I asked. "What's the battle they're fighting?"

"These women are in warfare for their lives!" said one of the hostesses, with a twinkle in her eye.

Having time on my hands, I decided to chat. "What does Mrs. Smith do with the ladies?" I asked.

"She tries a variety of things," said the plumper woman. "Once a month she has a craft class; sometimes, depending on the weather, she will rent a cabin in the park for a meeting then go outside awhile."

The other hostess joined the conversation. "Sometimes she gets a movie, or she shows exercise tapes and the women do exercises."

"It sounds like a good variety. What does she hope to accomplish in the women's group?" I asked.

"The basis for this women's support group is a holistic view. She takes the Word of God as the foundation and ties it with the Twelve Steps of AA. Through the discussions she shows them that they must find some of the sources for the addiction by letting the Word of God reveal some hidden truths to the women as to why they may have become addicted. They need to find release by learning about who they are and how they can handle their problems in this life, and not have their problems, pain, disappointments and broken dreams handle them."

Her friend took a turn explaining. "The Word of God gives the women a clear view of their lives. It changes the persons so that their view of the problems will not crush them, but supports them so much that they can work through the problems.They can also handle the day-to-day routines of life that women go through because they have a foundation to start from and stand on--the Word."

Irma came out from the office, greeted me, and called for us to come join her in prayer for Lillie and her two children. Both children had been outfitted with brand-new clothes, which I guessed had come from the back room. The little girl hugged her newly acquired teddy bear, which was almost as big as she, while the little brother tucked in his mother's arm drank milk from a bottle.

Gathering around this small family, we held hands as Irma prayed for Lillie in her new commitment to remain loyal to God and to her children. Tears streamed down the young mother's face as she prayed for wisdom and strength in her promise to serve God in this way.

Irma encouraged Lillie to join the women's support group."I want to see you here tomorrow morning if you are serious about choosing sobriety. It is the only way. You must determine in your mind that you can do it."

After many embraces and words of encouragement she left followed by the little girl who wore bright barrettes in her corn-rowed hair. One hand clutched her mother's skirt and the other dragged the teddy behind her.

As they started for the door Mrs. Davis reminded Lillie that she would be looking for her in the morning.

I turned to Mrs. Davis and said, "How soon after you started the Good News Club for children did you begin the women's support group?"

"It happened about the same time. I started attending all kind of seminars. As I attended those meetings I thought all the time about what I could do for my own people. I learned through the U.S. News and World Report back in 1989 that Youngstown is one of the worst small cities in the United States for its drug problems. I knew blacks were not comfortable going to all-white AA meetings, that it was necessary to start our own in the black community. It would work better if they themselves could be responsible for setting up the chairs, planning the meetings, and being a part of them.

"I saw we needed to help the youth before they got into trouble, and we needed to help detoxify people who had already gotten there. I got turned onto all our needs and what we should be doing."

Then in a contemplative mood Mrs. Davis said, "I was in the place in which Queen Esther found herself. She realized that if she didn't speak for her people they would all perish and that she would perish with them. She took courage and risked her life to save her people."

By now the "Warriors" had disbanded and Emaline Smith came over to join us.

"Do you have time to explain the Twelve Step program you use with the women?" I asked her.

"Sure. Let's go over to the classroom and I'll show you," she said as she pushed the room divider to the side. The other women excused themselves to return to their tasks.

"Before I tell you what we do, I'd like to give you some background about the Twelve Step program we use that was begun by Alcoholics Anonymous. AA started in Akron, Ohio, back in 1935 when an alcoholic businessman named Bill Wilson, who had sobered up after a conversion experience, came to Akron from New York and met Dr. Bob Smith, also a recovering alcoholic. The two teamed up to aid other persons who, like themselves, needed help staying sober. Wilson developed the Twelve Steps for recovery, which are now used all over the world. The AA headquarters is in New York City.

"We use the Twelve Steps as the basis for our recovery programs here at the Needle's Eye. In the first step the person has to admit he has a problem. We start each meeting in the same way: A person introduces him/herself by saying, 'I am Mary Smith and I am a recovering alcoholic.' If alcohol isn't the problem they may say, 'I'm a cocaine addict,' or 'I'm a narcotic addict,' but always admitting their problem.

"The second step is the idea of hope, or seeing the light. Third is the necessity of help from a higher power. We believe that God is present so we allow Him to work through us. The next steps involve confessing, making amends, continuing confirmation of the new person he/she has become, and redirecting energy to help others.

"One thing I must make clear. This is not a prayer meeting. It's a support group. We don't try to line the church pews with women from these meetings. Our purpose is to love them and meet their needs. We show them we care about them. How do I go about doing that? God reveals things to me.

"I find if I just talk to the women and go over the Twelve Steps together, we come upon their needs and know what to talk about. Each person has to follow each step. They're not allowed to skip any."

"We read the Twelve Steps out loud each time we meet, stopping to ask and answer questions.

"Where do all the women come from?" I asked.

"Some come on their own; other women are required to be at our meetings. If they have gone through court the judge sends them here; the women located at the rehab place are required to come. It's part of their discipline. We have to sign papers that they were present; they are checked out and if they don't show up they are investigated."

Mrs. Smith had more to say about the program. "The steps include a lot of spirituality along with them. Scripture passages are read right along with the discussion."

I pointed to the chalkboard:

>
> Acknowledge   Romans 3:23
>
> Repent   Luke 13:3
>
> Confess   I John 1:9
>
> Forsake   John 3:16
>
> Receive Power   John 1:12

"Those verses are the plan of salvation. Are you able to use them?" I asked.

She explained that she had used them with the lesson she had just finished.

"Today we covered step two," she said. "We talked about how a power greater than ourselves could restore us to sanity.' At this step we talked about the born-again experience. If you don't give people spirituality, then they are only dry drunks. There is no growth there. People must be growing in order to kick the habit.

"The counsellor's job is to bring that person to an understanding about the true and living God. If the counsellors don't know how to do that, then we have to train them.

"If you say, 'I don't want to bring religion into that, you lack understanding. I'm not religious, I'm a Christian! Do you know what a Christian is? The definition is to be Christlike.

"People accept the idea of God of the universe. If you talk about Jesus, a personal God, you can introduce them gently. It is so beautiful how these steps work!

"I tell them that life is full of hate, confusion and danger. Then, taking my Bible, I tell them to see what God's Word says. It says, 'I have love, peace and joy!'

"We take one step at a time and spend time on it until they are ready to move on. We take time for questions, maybe not answering them until the next meeting. We don't always talk--we also make soup, teach them how to quilt and how to care for a baby. That's how I handle the women. We treat it as a fireside chat."

"I see that you make yourself available to the women," I observed.

"They know if you care! I have to give of myself. It means running them around, visiting them in their homes, or answering the phone at night. But it has its rewards. When these women come here and become brand-new creatures in Christ Jesus, it's worth it all!"

Irma joined us, pointed to the poster about discipline and said. "That's what it takes: discipline, discipline, and more discipline! And that's one thing that is lacking in the homes.

"It's a hard thing to teach people responsibility if they haven't learned it at home, but we try. We point out to them that if they just show up we will try to help them. Often they feel like castaways. We say, 'God doesn't need your capability; he needs your availability. If people are willing to be helped, they'll move forward. It's a hard pull but they can make it, and we're here to help them!"

Chapter 13
"Youth Work"

It seemed everybody in Youngstown had turned out for the parade! Old folk leaning on canes, young married couples holding onto their children who were straining to step off the curb. Fathers hoisting babies on their shoulders. Everyone wanted to see all the way up and down Main Street. People were lined up from Market to Hillman.

There was an air of excitement as a band started playing in the distance. Floats started moving down the street, led by a clown strutting with a fistful of balloons. Next came members of the Needle's Eye youth group, all waving their homemade posters. I could read some of them: "Don't Drink and Drive" "Give Yourself Hope, Don't Use Dope". They chanted these slogans as they marched by.

The women "Warriors" came bearing a huge banner with glittering letters announcing the theme of the parade. No one could miss their bold message: "Say NO to Drugs and YES to Life!"

Afro-American youth, smiling and waving from inside decorated automobiles and vans, came riding next.

The South Side High School marching band was getting louder as it came into view--majorettes stepping high and twirling their batons, and instrumentalists in their red, white and blue uniforms, marched briskly to the rhythm of the music.

Youth in multi-colored T-shirts carefully lettered with anti-drug and alcohol slogans, the men's AA group, the Good News Club, PANDA--fifteen different organizations were marching, all representing the organization formed to wipe out alcoholism and use of drugs. They had come to make a statement to the city, and found an audience.

"You put a lot of work into this parade," I said as I turned to Irma and Bob.

"Not we alone, Celia. It was the youth who did most of the work. I organized it but they got into it and moved ahead," said Irma.

When the parade had passed the John Knox Church we turned and hurried toward the Needle's Eye just two blocks away. We would beat the parade and be ready to serve refreshments by the time they marched up Hillman and down Oak Hill to Kenmore.

"Having a parade has been a good activity for the youth," said Irma. "There is a lot of publicity. The mayor and city officials give the parade coverage in the news media. The parade trail goes right by the toughest part of town, past the worst pushers.

"A few years ago some pushers actually joined the parade, came to the Needle's Eye, saw the error of their ways and began the fight against drugs all because of our parade! So it's accomplishing its purpose. The parade creates a lot of excitement. I've got ideas already on how to sponsor the next one."

Once again I sensed the dynamics of a forceful leader such as my friend Irma. She has a goal and knows how to pursue it. I admired her honesty and openness and at the moment I wished for her stamina! I struggled to keep up with her as we walked briskly back to the Needle's Eye.

"Irma, I get the feeling that working with youth is a

priority in your life. Am I right?"

"Yes, it is the most important phase of my work," she said quickly. "Prevention rather than intervention" is a theme of mine. When youth get their mind on things other than alcohol and drugs and having sex--that's prevention.

"I'm thoroughly convinced that the way to help youth with the problems they face is to give them a better self-image, exposing them to Christian role models. This is ever so much more effective than trying to get them off drugs or alcohol. We aim to never let them start."

"That makes sense to me," I said, changing the subject. "Irma, what else goes on at the Needle's Eye today beside serving refreshments to everybody who comes?"

"There are speeches by important people talking to the youth; then if some of the teen-agers need transportation we'll see they get a way home."

It was later in the afternoon when the Davises and we were riding toward their house. Bob decided to show us the Mill Creek Park, one block from where they lived.

At the entrance to the park Bob pointed out the statue of Volney Rogers, founder of the park. "This park runs all the way through the city. Good highways make it easy to drive along the river. A few weeks ago it was the prettiest I've ever seen it. The leaves on the hardwood trees were so colorful. Most of them are down now."

Around every bend and over every hill there was another surprise.

"Over there--see that cabin?" asked Irma and pointing. "That's the place I often rent and bring the youth out here. It's where Emaline takes the women."

There was a surprising amount of lakes and waterfalls. Soon we passed Riverside Garden, Bear Hollow and Slippery Rock--a place with a large cabin on a slight hill. "The youth like that cabin," said Irma. "It has a big fireplace inside, a kitchen stove, tables that let down from the wall. There's a gold fish pond and lily park close by.

"When our son Ron went to college in Kansas, the folks

there couldn't believe that blacks could skate. He was the first black person to be on their ice hockey team. He learned to skate right here on the river. I took all the youth out to the park all the time. We'd go sledding, skating, tobogganing. In summer I'd take the youth group swimming, fishing, to play baseball, or soccer, or give them a hayride pulled by a tractor.

"Our family spent a lot of time doing things together down here. I'd cook a pot of beans and bring the kids to that picnic table over there by the river. Bob would meet us after work and we'd go fishing or hiking."

"Didn't the kids get lost?" I asked. "This park is huge!"

"I don't think there's a spot in this park I haven't been. I knew their favorite spots and I'd find them.

"There's Lincoln Park, Candall, Mill Creek, and Wick Park. I've taken the youth to all these.

"The youth groups used to know that I'd pray over them before I let them loose. When I'd forget they'd come up to me and bow their head and say, 'Mrs. Davis, you haven't prayed over us yet.'"

Bob stopped the car. "Calvin, I want to show you the rose garden. In summer it is a favorite place for people to come."

"Who takes care of the park?" asked Calvin.

"Mostly volunteers. Our children used to come here and help. We told them that they got a lot of good from Mill Park and they owed it to the city to help take care of it.

"Now it seems whenever our children come home with their children," he continued. "They always bring them down to the park just the way we used to take them."

I felt reluctant to leave the park. Its beauty was relaxing, but it was time to head for home. Calvin had to milk the cows and I had to prepare the Sunday school lesson for my adult class.

As Calvin and I headed west on Route 62 I fumbled through the tapes Irma had given me, popped the top one into the slot, and listened.

"I wonder who's talking on the tape," I said to Calvin.

"It must be their oldest son, Bob. Isn't he a youth minister?"

Needle's Eye

"I'm sure that's who it is," I said. "I remember Irma told me that after he served in the armed service, he rededicated his life to the Lord. Now he is married, has five children, and recently became a minister of the gospel in Baltimore, Maryland. He likes talking to youth.

"Irma told me he is their favorite speaker. Whenever she gives the young people in Youngstown a chance to choose a speaker they always choose him.

"I think maybe she was a bit prejudiced," I reasoned. "But she did say that the kids need a good role model to follow. One who follows Jesus, talks their language and understands their background.

"He probably has what it takes, if he follows his mom," said my husband.

With this in mind I decided to listen to the tapes analytically and see what Bob, Jr., did that appealed to youth.

He started with scripture or a Bible story; right away he involved his audience by asking questions. He gave a short lecture, then reinforced his theme with a short role-play or a story so the youth could apply the truth to their life. It was a good format.

I noticed that Rev. Davis talked so the youth could relate to his theme. On the tape "The Playground Is Closed," the scripture used was Exodus 32 in which the Children of Israel "rose up to play."

"That was all right at first," he said, "but they soon began to worship idols. They wandered from worship and only satisfied their lust."

He compared this to the playground between Hillman and Market Street that once had been a place for children to go to have fun. "Then drugs were brought in, as well as illicit sex, foul stories and stolen loot. The city had to come and close the playground," he said.

When I had time I listened to the rest of the tapes and videos; then I called Irma. "Who thinks of all the themes? Somebody's done some brainstorming to come up with those neat ideas!"

She laughed as she said, "I'm constantly on the lookout for what the youth need. Then I pray about it. The Lord never fails to give me an answer. Once while I was sick and lying on my back on the floor and looking up at the ceiling, I was praying to the Lord for a theme to better the youth's self-image. The thought came to me, 'We are never too far down that we can't look up!' That became the theme for the next seminar! Usually I tell the speakers what the theme is and they develop ideas for their talks. It works out."

"As I watched the videos of your camping experience I got the impression that the children were thoroughly enjoying themselves," I said to her. "I was impressed by the expertise of the counsellors in helping the children work through some delicate problems, like the small group that was doing puppets on the theme of child molestation. The counsellors were excellent in getting to the issues and giving help where it was needed."

"The counsellors are picked with great care," she said to me. "We have dedicated people, many of whom are professionals, who volunteer their time to come and help."

"The other videos were good too. I got a charge out of Bob working with the older teen-agers! He and the other man were role playing, pretending they didn't need discipline and that they got into trouble driving the car. They put in all the sound effects of a smash up that happened because they were drinking. I could see that would appeal to the youth.

"How often do you take the kids to camp?" I asked.

"Four times a year," came the quick reply. "We take them the day after Christmas, then in February in connection with the Black History month, the first week in June, and the longer experience in August. Bob usually comes for that one.

"Irma, do you go with them to camp?"

"Of course! I'm still a kid at heart myself. I love going out-of-doors and I think there's no better place to get close to God than out in nature, so I go with the campers. They love being there! After all, being cooped up in the city--who wouldn't like it? This is the only vacation some of them get; they get to try new things.

"The reason I like taking them is it gets the kids away from their environment to learn something good, to see that there is a better way of life. It gives them a brand-new value system. If they only see drug and alcohol abuse they won't know there is another way. We teach them about Jesus. We teach them Bible verses and how to pray. I try to think of all the things I used to do with my kids that worked--things they liked to do.

"There is something about being in camp that gets you close to the kids. When you eat and sleep with them you know what they're thinking and you can help them. We talk to them and tell them they can be proud of their heritage and that they are somebody. Then they'll listen to you."

"Hey! You're right on!" I said enthusiastically. "Irma, you don't do all this by yourself, do you?"

"I used to try that, but it got to be too much. No, I make everybody help. For instance, when we have cultural youth camp, the youth from the Needle's Eye act as hosts to all the rest of the campers who come from Warren, Cleveland, Dayton, and Baltimore, Maryland. They are responsible for welcoming everybody, and making them comfortable by showing them the cabins. They are in charge of making the kids stick with the rules. Everybody who's coming to camp knows the rules. I send many letters getting them ready for camp long ahead of time. If anyone gets out of line at camp my kids report it to me immediately. They know I don't fool around. If they deliberately act up, I warn them, and if they don't change I call their parents and they are sent home. If their parents don't come for them, we take them home and they are not allowed ever to come to camp again. That's it and they know it.

"Do you want to hear of our latest innovation?" asked Mrs. Davis. I could sense the excitement in her voice.

"Tell me."

"You know of the Laubach method of learning? Where each one teaches one?"

"Yes, I'm familiar with it."

"We've invited potential leaders from all over to our next camp session. Some are coming from Maryland, some from

Pennsylvania, and from the big cities in Ohio. The organizations they represent pick the kids who show potential leadership ability. We'll get them together in a training seminar on sexuality. We'll get the best speakers possible and we hope that these kids will go back home and teach other kids what they learned.

"Besides the lecture we'll give them all kind of physical activities, such as swimming, dancing, hiking, basketball and good food! I have a list of churches willing to supply the meals."

"Sounds great!"

"We'll have sit-down meals, family style. Lots of these kids never have this on a regular basis; some never heard of it."

"Do you know what, Irma? After watching the videos and seeing what you do with kids at camp, I wouldn't mind stopping in to observe."

"Come ahead! You won't even have to go far. I've planned to go to a Mennonite camp near Kidron called Camp Luz."

"Really? Camp Luz? That's a beautiful spot. It has a lake, and a long drive with the cabins nestled in a wooded area. They have a big dining hall, a chapel, all kinds of facilities for physical activities, a loft built in a big oak to watch the birds. The kids will love it!

"The number who plan to come keeps growing. I thought maybe twenty but already thirty have registered.

When the big weekend arrived I could see that a lot of preparation had gone into the program. Forty youth showed up!

I stopped in periodically to see the progress. Whenever I did, Irma would stop and talk. "For this seminar the kids were screened. We're making an investment and expecting results. Take a look at their schedule."

"Whew! You're really packing a lot into a short weekend!" I whistled. "You really keep them hopping!"

"That's part of our strategy. We keep them so busy they don't have time to get into any trouble. Our ratio for counsellors to campers is three to one."

The campers were milling around to get acquainted with each other. Suddenly I noticed a disruption. Evidently one of the boys had made a snide remark about another boy's hairdo. There was tussling and pushing. The boy whose head was shaven clean except for the hair on the very top of his head was trying to sock the offender.

Quick as a wink, the youth leader brought the boys to Irma. She looked at them and glared. "What's going on?" she demanded.

They told her. "Well, apologize!" she said. The boys apologized in front of the group that had gathered. Soon the two were playing ball together.

"You have to handle those things right away," she said. "If you let them go it only leads to trouble."

"I found that out teaching school," I replied. "Kids like to know where they stand; limits create security."

As I observed the group in action I saw that the counselors were willing to share on personal levels of their own sexuality to give the campers confidence in speaking of their experiences. I saw Irma trying the new dance to break the ice when the campers felt intimidated. Gradually the campers followed the leaders skilled in creative arts, in thought processes, challenging the campers in a talent show that turned out to be a riot of fun!

"You know what I'm planning for the next time we have such a seminar?" Irma asked me. "We've got to cover all aspects of our culture: ethnic foods, music, dress, literature, and artifacts," she said scanning her imaginary list. "These kids have to know where they come from in order for them to know where they are going."

"How are you going to work it?"

"Usually I come up with a topic, then discuss it with the youth leaders. They say what they would like to see on the program, then check it out with me. I, in turn, make suggestions or name possible speakers. They affirm or reject my ideas. We negotiate until we have an agreement. I find that the youth are more willing to help and take leadership roles if they have had a part in the planning."

"What are your goals for this particular seminar?" I asked.

"This one is aimed at sexuality. It is our hope that these

kids will go back to their communities and share what they learned here this weekend. Another time we will take another topic and in that way get the message back to those needing to hear it. What do you think?"

"The idea is terrific! Absolutely terrific!"

Chapter 14
"Models"

Two men came into the Needle's Eye just as I was about to finish one of my periodic visits. Mrs. Davis introduced them to me. "This is Joe. He used to be an alcoholic. How many years are you in sobriety?" "It's been fifteen years since I was delivered," he replied, his face beaming. "This man has helped masses of people in the three-county area in getting them in for counsel. Ah-my!! He knows how to work a program to help people. How the Lord has used him!" Irma said.

Joe turned and introduced his friend Bob to Mrs. Davis. When everyone was acquainted, she continued her conversation with Joe. "How are things going?" she asked. Then, turning to me, she explained, "Joe works full time in social services. On his days off, he used to come and help us; now he goes to different areas that have started counseling centers and he gets people into the program."

"Things are going quite well, thank you," said Joe. "Not all the programs are working as well as yours here in Youngstown. Do you remember when I worked here how we discussed the financial support system of the Needle's Eye?" "That's an important phase of running a program," said Mrs. Davis. "Well, some of the new places try to run the program pretty much on their own. They don't use a board to help raise money, to determine how much money to spend, and how to spend it . . ."

"Listen, I give an account for everything down to the last dime!" said Mrs. Davis. "I get receipts for all my expenditures, and I want it that way! The board members represent the churches that support us. They have a right to know! Many programs fall by the wayside because they don't have financial discipline."

"How many churches are represented on your board?" I asked.

"We get most of our money from the East Presbytery. The Presbyterian, Lutheran, Episcopal, Free Methodist, Methodist, Baptists, Catholic and Evangelical churches give regular support; then there are others who send donations such as the Mennonite Sunday school class who sent us money for a phone when we needed that service."

"That's quite a variety," I said. "You need that. The members who make up the board are lawyers, CPA's, school teachers, nurses, lay members. There are twenty-two members on our board; they meet once every month to determine what we should be doing, they handle all the money . . ."

Irma paused a moment, then added, "I've decided that in order to be a good leader I have to be a good follower. If I expect people under me to follow my instructions, then I'd better be willing to listen to somebody over me and comply with their wishes."

She turned to the men and said, "There's another city interested in starting a program similar to ours." "Where is that?" asked Joe. "The folks at Newport News, Virginia asked me to come with my staff and present a seminar. "Really? Down in the Tidewater Valley? They want to start a program like the one you have here?" asked Joe's friend.

"Yes, they are, but let me explain the way it was. Those people had a plan to evangelize their city. They strategized by having churches throughout the city adopt their own territory, committing themselves to help meet the social and spiritual needs of that area.

"They had an advisory board of operation which gave support to the churches with the training and guidance necessary to keep the program going.

"The leader of the board needed some input on helping the churches understand how to address the drug and alcohol problem, so he asked us to come to present a seminar on how we do it here in Youngstown."

"How did they know about your program?" asked Joe.

"The leader heard me speak at a seminar in Baltimore, Maryland, and asked me to come."

"Baltimore, Maryland? Where else have you gone to present seminars?" I asked.

"There have been a few others; twice I went to Baltimore, and to Kent, Ravenna, Windom, and lots of them here in Youngstown. "Irma, let's suppose a city wants to start a program similar to what you have here at the Needle's Eye; what are the steps needed in doing that?" I asked. She responded quickly.

"First, the local folks have to find out what the needs are in _their_ city. People living in a community know the needs. Here in Youngstown we wanted to solve the drug problem. In another city it may be a feeding program for malnutrition, an adult literacy program for the illiterate, a vocational school to teach skills, or whatever the need is.

"Once the problem is identified, a group of community people get together and discuss what they intend to do. They lay out their goals, check out alternative plans, and then go about implementing them."

"In your case, you and your neighbors sensed the drug and alcohol problem." "Right. But first we prayed about it. That's always the first step and the most important one! You need to feel the Holy Spirit's leading before you do anything else."

Encouraging her to keep talking, I said, "You started attending seminars to learn all you could. Once you sensed a solution, you talked to other people about starting a counselling center."

"Right. I picked up literature and books and everything I could lay my hands on to learn all I could about it. For example, every major city has a directory of recovery services. You need to know that in order to find where to send people. Every city has organizations that willingly channel into your program once it's started, such as referrals from judges, the parole system, children's services, juvenile research center, jails, prisons, rehabilitation and detoxification centers, and churches."

"Then you get financial support. You already named your sources," I said. "In our case the churches gave not only monetary support but they helped make soup, set up learning centers and provided volunteers to help us."

"I'm impressed that it takes a lot of people to run a place like the Needle's Eye," I suggested.

"You better believe it!" replied Mrs. Davis. "I saw I couldn't do it alone. The Lord showed me the people who were qualified and I'd ask them for help."

"Irma, you mentioned a few other groups who have started programs similar to what you have here at the Needle's Eye. Could I talk to someone who has started a program patterned after the Needle's Eye? Who has started a program and would be able to tell me about their procedure?"

"You could call Gary Hamm in Newport News, Virginia. He coordinated 'Operation: Breaking Through' in that city; but he's hard to catch. You'd have to call him early in the morning.

I called Mr. Hamm at six in the morning and found his voice brisk and cheerful. After identifying myself I said, "I'm writing a book about Irma Davis in Youngstown, Ohio, and am seeing her program a model-one others can use to start a Christian counselling center. She gave me a copy of your 'Adopt-a-Community' plan. I was impressed by your strategy." I continued to explain my purpose in calling. "It is my understanding that you use each of the fifteen churches in your area to adopt and to be committed to a given section of your city to help solve problems. What are the key ingredients in implementing a program that will work? One that will bring about desired changes?"

This man of God sensed what I wanted. He began by explaining the motivating force behind the program. "The city is the heart of God," he said. It's the place where most people live. It's the center of power and God is in the heart of it. He has established a beachhead. The way to mobilize people is to love God actively. This compelling force will awaken people's lives. "In the Bible Jesus asked Peter three times if he loved Him. 'Lovest thou me?' he asked Peter. If you love God, you'll love His work. You'll get excited about the relationship with Him. You'll just naturally reach out to others. "In John 10 Jesus said, 'Other sheep I have which are not of this fold. Them also I must bring. They, too, shall hear my voice and they shall be one fold and one shepherd. "God is the chief shepherd. The pastor is the under-shepherd. In order to serve, one must be willing to be a servant! A servant to the community is a local tenant clothed in servant roles. "The pastor gears his efforts towards church people. In order to mobilize the church you must develop relationships with people. In order to make disciples you must be a friend and have relationships with people. "Housing and social services are all right, but if the heart isn't in it, it is not effective. If people get involved, then things begin to change.

Until you meet the felt needs of people, you won't earn the right to help people. It needs to be a holistic approach. Meeting felt needs is first. Establish an agenda second. Each church that adopts a community is accountable to that. My job as coordinator means I use all the various churches to allow them to work within their own jurisdiction. No church loses its identity. Two ingredients are:the program must be, one, community-based, and, two, Christ-centered. Whatever the program, whether its a girls' charm school, et cetera, we let them work to mobilize our city in the ways the Spirit brings it to them.

"You must mix church and state affairs. It is more than a social problem; it is also a religious problem. You need the religious coalition. In 'Operation: Breaking Through,' we are using fifteen churches.

"Churches must never be patronizing. We must always accept others as human beings, no matter how bad off they are!

We need to affirm their dignity and love them. "Jesus touched people. He acknowledged them and built a relationship. That is what it means in Romans: 'I have become all things to all people in order that I may win some to Christ.' "When our city was developing our program and we were considering substance abuse, I remembered the seminar in Baltimore, Maryland, where Irma Davis spoke. I felt we needed her expertise. We invited and paid expenses for her to come. The churches worked together and gave us our impetus to propel the operation. Even the mayor came to bless it!

"Irma Davis, as I said, is a master in the kingdom of God. She has a right to help people because she has established a relationship with them. One former mayor's life was changed after she was touched by Irma's faith.

"Mrs. Davis has been a prevention specialist. She emphasizes helping the youth before they get into trouble. She knows how to motivate people, secure speakers, and she is a caring counsellor. We are reproducing what Irma's doing in the Needle's Eye. It is another fruit of her ministry. "There is a slogan she created when she was still in high school," I said. "I think it is one we could all adopt:" I paused. "What is it? he prodded.

"I was born not for myself only, but for the good of the world," I quoted. "That pretty well sums up the philosophy of Irma Davis' life," he said. We both agreed.

Epilogue

The 1990's are rough! Murder is an everyday occurrence in Youngstown, Ohio. Teenagers can't find work, children are being battered, people are angry enough to kill. Children are having babies so therefore there is no maturity. Some thirty-year-old women don't know the name of their mother or father. If they don't know where they come from, how can they know where they are going?

Sometimes Irma Davis feels she is losing the battle in this jungle of sin. But just when she gets discouraged the Lord sends messages of hope through the scripture. Recently she was inspired by the promise in II Kings 3:16: "This is what the Lord says: Make this valley full of ditches." She envisioned irrigation ditches with Christ's love and gentleness flowing in a continuous stream into a parched land. The message was clear. Instead of beating down the jungle; she would irrigate the land.

She set forth with new vigor to minister to the mother of the fifteen-year-old son who killed two men the same night. She found ways of working with the rebellious drug-addicted children who lack adequate education. There are words of encouragement for the fearful teen-agers who find the only job available is selling drugs and becoming a part of another kind of slavery. She learned not to fight back when a man in a stick up ran off with her suitcases full of clothing.

She sees the effects of the "watering" of gentleness in love as she presents a seminar and suddenly a lady jumps to her feet and says, "I want to know Jesus." Irma stops her lecture and explains salvation and nine people respond to a new life in Christ.

Hope rises when the little boys say to Ronald Foreman, one of the volunteer workers at the Needle's Eye, "I wish you were my daddy."

Irma Davis has become so involved in the lives of her people that when she received a call from the White House to be saluted by President Bush for the one hundred seventy-sixth "Daily Point of Light," she sent her son Bob Davis residing in Baltimore to go in her place. Though she does not seek publicity, she felt honored to be recognized as being successful in providing counselling and rehabilitation through a variety of programs for problems related to drug and alcohol abuse.

Irma finally met President George Bush at Canton, Ohio airport.